BATTLE FOR BRITAIN

"A goblet," said Arthu
gold cup is much more—
the power to change histo
mac Llyr must find it, wl
failed.

The search leads to highwaymen, the cursed un-
dead, witchcraft, and nightmares from the depths of
lore. Further, Niall must join, or battle, the champi-
ons Mael mac Ronan, Starkad the Dane, and the
sorceress Veleda—who believe the fate of the world
depends on Arthur *not* finding the cup.

And if Niall finds the cup? Will preserving Arthur's
dream create a brutal, eternal empire? Will defeating
Merlin's vision plunge Britain into a dark age of
chaos? Will the goblet save Camelot—or destroy the
world?

CROSSROADS™ ADVENTURES are authorized interactive novels compatible for Advanced Dungeons
and Dragons™ level play. Constructed by the masters
of modern gaming, CROSSROADS™ feature complete rules; *full use* of gaming values—strength,
intelligence, wisdom/luck, constitution, dexterity,
charisma, and hit points; and multiple pathways for
each option, for the most complete experience in
gaming books, as fully realized, motivated heroes
quest through the most famous worlds of fantasy!

All-New. With an Introduction
by David Drake
ENTER THE ADVENTURE!

Advanced Dungeons and Dragons™ is a trademark of
TSR, Inc.

TOR'S CROSSROADS ADVENTURE SERIES

Dragonharper, based on Anne McCaffrey's Pern
Storm of Dust, based on David Drake's The Dragon Lord
Revolt on Majipoor, based on Robert Silverberg's Majipoor

COMING SOON

The Witchfires of Leth, based on C.J. Cherryh's Morgaine
Prospero's Isle, based on L. Sprague de Camp and
    Fletcher Pratt's The Incomplete Enchanter
Dzurlord, based on Steven Brust's Jhereg
A Warlock's Blade, based on Christopher Stasheff's
    Gramarye
Encyclopedia of Xanth, based on Piers Anthony's Xanth
Warhorn, based on Lynn Abbey's Rifkind

A CROSSROADS ADVENTURE

in the World of
DAVID DRAKE'S DRAGON LORD
STORM OF DUST

by
Neil Randall

A TOM DOHERTY ASSOCIATES BOOK

First printing: August 1987

A TOR Book

Published by Tom Doherty Associates, Inc.
49 West 24 Street
New York, N.Y. 10010

Cover art by Doug Beekman
Illustrations by Todd Cameron Hamilton

ISBN: 0-812-56400-6
CAN. ED.: 0-812-56401-4

Printed in the United States of America

0 9 8 7 6 5 4 3 2 1

This book is dedicated to my wife, Heather, and my daughters, Catherine and Michelle, for their unfailing support.

Special thanks to Gerry Klug, who gave me a chance in the beginning; to my parents, for their constant help; and to John Bell, for making myth real.

STORM OF DUST:
AN INTRODUCTION
by David Drake

I WOUND UP writing *The Dragon Lord* because I hadn't been interested in ever doing a novel about King Arthur.

Which is not to say that I wasn't interested in King Arthur. I'd read tales of Arthur and his knights when I was too young to recall the author. I have vivid—imagined—recollections of men standing bone-weary at sundown, their shields hacked to splinters and their helmets battered from their heads . . . knowing that at dawn they will fight again, for another day and for as many days as it takes before one or the other of them is defeated. Howard Pyle? Perhaps; certainly I read Pyle's retellings in later years.

When I was fourteen I got—bless the Teen-Age Book Club—a paperback of Malory's *Le Morte d'Arthur*. I read the volume and reread it, wondering whether a palfrey was a horse or a donkey . . . wondering about many words and usages, and utterly charmed by the self-consistent fantasy world within the pages of that book.

Malory's a good place to have been, because he's as

much the beginning of Arthurian literature as Bram Stoker began vampire literature. There was vampire fiction before *Dracula*; but every writer on the subject today must consciously accept or reject Stoker.

The same is true of Malory. A decade or so later I read *Sir Gawain and the Green Knight* and Chretien of Troyes' *Arthurian Romances*. More recently still, Penguin Books has reprinted translations of anonymous Arthurian epics. These fictions must have influenced Malory, but I don't think they affected *The Dragon Lord* except at secondhand—through *Le Morte d'Arthur*.

There are few historical sources covering Britain at the time of Arthur. Most of the references which exist are very brief ones; I defy anyone to pad the two paragraphs in Gildas, for instance, into a novel. Geoffrey of Monmouth deals with Arthur at length, but the subject is as much a fictional creation as the hero of the romances of Wace and Layamon.

By the spring of 1977, I'd read the pre-modern historical references to Arthur as well as the medieval romances on the subject which had come to hand. To me, Arthur was still Malory's creation, and my reading was purely for pleasure. I had no desire to rewrite *Le Morte d'Arthur*.

Which made Arthur the perfect subject for me when Andy Offutt offered to pay me for plotting a novel to be set in 500 A.D. or thereabouts.

Andy was doing a series of novels continuing the adventures of Cormac mac Art, one of the less successful characters created by Robert E. Howard. Cormac was in the mold of Conan or King Kull; but, unlike them, he was an Irishman of the fifth century A.D. instead of a character set in a mythical past.

For my own part, I was an attorney who had been writing and selling occasional stories as a hobby since 1965. I was beginning to achieve some success with science fiction, but my first love was sword and sorcery pieces with meticulously researched historical settings. Short story markets for that sort of thing were few and far between, and I hadn't any notion of how one went about structuring a novel.

Andy had bought a couple of my stories for collections which he edited. The research, at least, had impressed him, and I was one of several people whom he contacted to do backgrounds and plots for him on the Cormac series.

I was delighted. The best part of the arrangement was not the pay (unspecified, but surely insignificant compared to what I earned as a lawyer) or even the offer of a credit line if my work justified it. Rather, it was the chance to see how an experienced novelist would convert my outline into a full-length novel. My longest piece at that time was about 10,000 words, and the difference between that and 80,000 is mind-boggling until you've been there once or twice.

Just as the pay wasn't the real incentive for me to take on the job, neither was the work itself the downside of the arrangement. I was worried that I would lose the plot of a book that I would want to write some day when I had learned *how* to write novels.

But that was catch-22. I'd tried several times to write full-length novels and had run out of steam each time. I was going to have to sacrifice a plot in order to learn how to write novels myself.

I got down to work by rereading Howard's Cormac mac Art stories. I've been a Howard fan at least since

1958, when I bought an Ace paperback of *Conan the Conqueror*. The Howard boom of the '70s resurrected a great deal of material which would have remained buried if it hadn't been written by the creator of Conan. Much of the material was juvenile; some of it was fragmentary; and most of it had proven to be unsalable in the 1930s, when the standards of publishable fiction were lower than they have become since the demise of the pulps.

The Cormac mac Art stories suffered under all three heads. They were bad stories, redeemed by having been the training ground for one of the best commercial storytellers of this century. I'd read them initially for pleasure—and had found pleasure in them, despite their awkwardness. I reread them, looking for a hook on which to hang a plot—and found not only that but also a way out of my concern over 'losing' a subject I might one day wish to treat in a novel of my own.

Two of the Cormac stories made passing reference to King Arthur. I could bring Cormac into the court of King Arthur, using the realistic fifth-century background in which Howard had placed his character instead of the medieval legend which Malory had created.

I knew I'd *never* want to write a novel about King Arthur myself.

Besides the original Cormac stories, I read Andy's first novel in the series and his outline for the next one. That gave me a notion of what he would need from me, and it also provided me with the cast of continuing characters.

Howard had introduced a huge Danish axeman,

Wulfhere the Skullsplitter, into some of the stories. He was now a permanent fixture. In addition, Andy had provided Cormac with a female companion and also with a Druid to handle magical chores.

Then I got down to the real business, researching a setting of which I knew almost nothing. I don't say "the real work" because it was genuine fun, the sort of thing that I love to do.

The only secondary source which I used extensively was *The Age of Arthur* by John Morris. He organizes the written history regarding the British Isles during the period 350–650 A.D. and fleshes it out with the results of modern scholarship and archeological research. The result is a thoroughly interesting book, but it had much less effect on the way I plotted the novel than I had expected it would.

Morris says in his Introduction, "The personality of Arthur is unknown and unknowable." The novel I plotted—every work of fiction I have plotted before then or since—would be about people, not events. Morris's expert catalog of real events and the evidence for them was as foreign to my purpose as was Malory's tapestry of characters in timeless legend.

I gained one scrap of insight from a secondary source which was of great importance to me as I plotted the novel. Until a moment ago, I thought the source was Morris—but that appears not to be the case.

The information is straightforward. The sixth-century Byzantine historian Procopius explains that Italy in his day had a serious problem with German immigration. Excess population from northern Germany, which for generations had been absorbed by Britain, now began to seek living room in Italy.

I'd read that passage myself, but I did not realize its implication until someone else—wish I could remember his or her name—drew my attention to it: somebody in Britain around 500 A.D. was making it impossible for Germans to take British land for themselves as they had been doing during past decades.

His name may not have been Arthur, but there was *some* British warlord kicking ass and taking names among the invaders who'd had everything their own way for so long. Everything written about King Arthur, including his name, might be fictional; but the man himself was as real as Julius Caesar. That made a difference in how I viewed the character who would otherwise have remained a fragment of Malory's legendry in my mind.

What I found I wanted in written sources were things that gave me the *feel* of a period very different from our own. The three sources which proved most valuable to me were:

1) *Beowulf.* I've loved this work since I was seven years old or thereabouts and read a serialized version of it in *Jack & Jill* magazine. The serial was very well written and may have shaped *The Dragon Lord* as much as did my many later readings of the poem in translation. The serial—and not any of the translations I have since read—referred to shields made of yellow linden wood. In homage to that memory, I repeated the phrase in my novel.

The poem itself was composed by an anonymous Anglo-Saxon in the ninth century, but it deals with events of approximately the period I wanted. At least one of the characters in *Beowulf* was a historical figure who was killed in 521 A.D. The opinions of a settled poet about how his ancestors thought and behaved three centuries earlier may not be wholly authoritative, but they were valid enough for my purposes.

2) *The History of the Danes* by an anonymous Saxon grammarian (*Saxo Grammaticus* in the Latin in which he wrote his history). This work provided useful bits of data—for instance, the Irish practice of strewing spikes, caltrops, on the ground to break up the dense formations of armored Norsemen.

More important to my plot and the way it developed were some specific incidents which I used entire. The most striking of these was the account of two friends who vowed to be buried together. When one died, the other joined him in his barrow; but the "dead" man came alive during the night and pursued his former friend within the tomb until grave robbers opened it.

3) *The Histories of the Wars* by the sixth-century Byzantine historian Procopius, describing the campaigns of his master, Belisarius, against Vandals, Goths, and Franks. This is an account by a man who was prescient of the way a small professional army could defeat much larger armies of Germans. The crucial elements were archers, mounted on horses and equipped with heavy armor.

We have no hard evidence on what Arthur's army looked like. We do know what kind of army Belisarius used to defeat similar German opponents a generation later. I believe that Arthur's forces were of the same pattern, because I cannot conceive of any other kind of force that would have permitted him to achieve what he did with the limited available resources.

But the man who welded the defeated, fragmented Britons into a fighting force that stopped and then threw back the hordes of conquering Germans could not have been a wistful dreamer. He must have been a very hard man, as terrible as he was great; and it was that realization, not my previous intention, which caused me to describe the King Arthur of my novel in the fashion I did.

I modeled the personality of my character on the merged personalities of two great leaders with whom I had some familiarity: Alexander the Great and Adolf Hitler.

Apart from reading, my wife and I visited England that summer. I bought books, took notes and photographs, and had an altogether great time. (This isn't a foolproof way to gather data. I misunderstood a guide's mention of the weeping beech at Stoke Poges. The weeping beech we planted in our yard when we got back is never going to grow tall enough to shelter three adults the way the tree in *The Dragon Lord* does.)

So, for five months I assembled material, organized it, and turned it into an outline of 16,000 words—which Andy Offutt, as it turned out, no longer needed.

There'd been problems with the publisher of the Cormac series (it was later moved to another house), and others had provided Andy with satisfactory plots much more quickly than I could manage. He was perfectly fair about the matter, offering to pay me for the outline with the intention of recasting it as a sword and planet novel at some future date.

But a funny thing had happened while I worked on the outline: I'd come to love the subject in a way I hadn't dreamed I would. I was delighted to tell Andy that he needn't pay me: I would write the novel myself.

And I did.

Not in the series, of course. *Cormac mac Art: The Dragon Lord* became simply *The Dragon Lord*. I combined Andy's female character and the Druid into a single personage—the Veleda. She was a hereditary prophet of the Bructeri during the first century A.D.—of whom nothing is known beyond a few lines in Tacitus' *Histories*. I hope my usage did no injustice to her.

The other main characters of *The Dragon Lord*, Mael and Starkad, are Robert E. Howard's Cormac and Wulfhere. I've never, strictly speaking, written a pastiche of another author's work; but this, my first novel, is a pastiche in everything but the names of the characters.

Occasionally I'm asked if I'll write a sequel to *The Dragon Lord*. No, I don't think so. But I have a great deal of affection for Mael, Starkad, and Veleda. We went through a lot together; and, in the way they launched my writing career, they proved to be as good a trio of friends to me as they are to each other.

David Drake
Chapel Hill, NC

INTRODUCTION AND RULES TO CROSSROADS™ ADVENTURES
by Bill Fawcett

FOR THE MANY of us who have enjoyed the stories upon which this adventure is based, it may seem a bit strange to find an introduction this long at the start of a book. What you are holding is both a game and an adventure. Have you ever read a book and then told yourself you would have been able to think more clearly or seen a way out of the hero's dilemma? In a Crossroads™ adventure you have the opportunity to do just that. *You* make the key decisions. By means of a few easily followed steps you are able to see the results of your choices.

A Crossroads™ adventure is as much fun to read as it is to play. It is more than just a game or a book. It is a chance to enjoy once more a familiar and treasured story. The excitement of adventuring in a beloved universe is neatly blended into a story which stands well on its own merit, a story in which you will encounter many familiar characters and places and discover more than a few new ones as well. Each adventure is a thrilling tale, with the extra suspense and satisfaction of knowing that you will succeed or fail by your own endeavors.

THE ADVENTURE

Throughout the story you will have the opportunity to make decisions. Each of these decisions will affect whether *the hero* succeeds in the quest, or even survives. In some cases you will actually be fighting battles; other times you will use your knowledge and instincts to choose the best path to follow. In many cases there will be clues in the story or illustrations.

A Crossroads™ adventure is divided into sections. The length of a section may be a few lines or many pages. The section numbers are shown at the top of a page to make it easier for you to follow. Each section ends when you must make a decision, or fight. The next section you turn to will show the results of your decision. At least one six-sided die and a pencil are needed to "play" this book.

The words "six-sided dice" are often abbreviated as "D6." If more than one is needed a number will precede the term. "Roll three six-sided dice" will be written as roll "3 D6." Virtually all the die rolls in these rules do involve rolling three six-sided dice (or rolling one six-sided die three times) and totaling what is rolled.

If you are an experienced role-play gamer, you may also wish to convert the values given in this novel to those you can use with TSR's Advanced Dungeons and Dragons™ or any other role-playing game. All of the adventures have been constructed so that they also can be easily adapted in this manner. The values for the hero will transfer directly. While AD & D™ games are much more complicated, doing this will allow you to be the Game Master for other players. Important values for the hero's opponents will be given to aid you in this conversion and to give those playing by the Crossroads™ rules a better idea of what they are facing.

THE HERO

Seven values are used to describe the hero in gaming terms. These are strength, intelligence, wisdom/luck, constitution, dexterity, charisma, and hit points. These values measure all of a character's abilities. At the end of these rules is a record sheet. On it are given all of the values for the hero of this adventure and any equipment or supplies they begin the adventure with. While you adventure, this record can be used to keep track of damage received and any new equipment or magical items acquired. You may find it advisable to make a photocopy of that page. Permission to do so, for your own use only, is given by the publisher of this game/novel. You may wish to consult this record sheet as we discuss what each of the values represents.

STRENGTH

This is the measure of how physically powerful your hero is. It compares the hero to others in how much the character can lift, how hard he can punch, and just how brawny he is. The strongest a normal

human can be is to have a strength value of 18. The
weakest a child would have is a 3. Here is a table
giving comparable strengths:

Strength	Example
3	A five-year-old child
6	An elderly man
8	Out of shape and over 40
10	An average 20-year-old man
13	In good shape and works out
15	A top athlete or football running back
17	Changes auto tires without a jack
18	Arm wrestles Arnold Schwarzenegger and wins

A Tolkien-style troll, being magical, might have a
strength of 19 or 20. A full-grown elephant has a
strength of 23. A fifty-foot dragon would have a
strength of 30.

INTELLIGENCE

Being intelligent is not just a measure of native
brain power. It is also an indication of the ability to
use that intelligence. The value for intelligence also
measures how aware the character is, and so how
likely they are to notice a subtle clue. Intelligence
can be used to measure how resistant a mind is to
hypnosis or mental attack. A really sharp baboon
would have an intelligence of 3. Most humans (we all
know exceptions) begin at about 5. The highest value
possible is an 18. Here is a table of relative intelligence:

Intelligence	Example
3	My dog
5	Lassie
6	Curly (the third Stooge)
8	Somewhat slow
10	Average person
13	College professor/good quarterback
15	Indiana Jones/Carl Sagan
17	Doc Savage/Mr. Spock
18	Leonardo da Vinci (Isaac Asimov?)

Brainiac of comic-book fame would have a value of 21.

WISDOM/LUCK

Wisdom is the ability to make correct judgments, often with less than complete facts. Wisdom is knowing what to do and when to do it. Attacking, when running will earn you a spear in the back, is the best part of wisdom. Being in the right place at the right time can be called luck or wisdom. Not being discovered when hiding can be luck, but if it is because you knew enough to not hide in the poison oak, wisdom is also a factor. Activities which are based more on instinct, the intuitive leap, than analysis are decided by wisdom.

In many ways both wisdom and luck are further connected, especially as wisdom also measures how friendly the ruling powers of the universe (not the author, the fates) are to the hero. A hero may be favored by fate or luck because he is reverent or for no discernible reason at all. This will give him a high wisdom value. Everyone knows those "lucky" individuals who can fall in the mud and find a gold coin. Here is a table measuring relative wisdom/luck:

Wisdom	Example
Under 3	Cursed or totally unthinking
5	Never plans, just reacts
7	Some cunning, "street smarts"
9	Average thinking person
11	Skillful planner, good gambler
13	Successful businessman/Lee Iacocca
15	Captain Kirk (wisdom)/Conan (luck)
17	Sherlock Holmes (wisdom)/Luke Skywalker (luck)
18	Lazarus Long

CONSTITUTION

The more you can endure, the higher your constitution. If you have a high constitution you are better able to survive physical damage, emotional stress, and poisons. The higher your value for constitution, the longer you are able to continue functioning in a difficult situation. A character with a high constitution can run farther (though not necessarily faster) or hang by one hand longer than the average person. A high constitution means you also have more stamina, and recover more quickly from injuries. A comparison of values for constitution:

Constitution	Example
3	A terminal invalid
6	A ten-year-old child
8	Your stereotyped "98-pound weakling"
10	Average person
14	Olympic athlete/Sam Spade
16	Marathon runner/Rocky
18	Rasputin/Batman

A whale would have a constitution of 20. Superman's must be about 50.

DEXTERITY

The value for dexterity measures not only how fast a character can move, but how well-coordinated those movements are. A surgeon, a pianist, and a juggler all need a high value for dexterity. If you have a high value for dexterity you can react quickly (though not necessarily correctly), duck well, and perform sleight-of-hand magic (if you are bright enough to learn how). Conversely, a low dexterity means you react slowly and drop things frequently. All other things being equal, the character with the highest dexterity will have the advantage of the first attack in a combat. Here are some comparative examples of dexterity:

Dexterity	Example
3 or less	Complete klutz
5	Inspector Clousseau

6	Can walk and chew gum, most of the time
8	Barney Fife
10	Average person
13	Good fencer/Walter Payton
15	Brain surgeons/Houdini
16	Flying Karamazov Brothers
17	Movie ninja/Cyrano de Bergerac
18	Bruce Lee

Batman, Robin, Daredevil, and The Shadow all have a dexterity of 19. At a dexterity of 20 you don't even see the man move before he has taken your wallet and underwear and has left the room (the Waco Kid).

CHARISMA

Charisma is more than just good looks, though they certainly don't hurt. It is a measure of how persuasive a hero is and how willing others are to do what he wants. You can have average looks yet be very persuasive, and have a high charisma. If your value for charisma is high, you are better able to talk yourself out of trouble or obtain information from a stranger. If your charisma is low, you may be ignored or even mocked, even when you are right. A high charisma value is vital to entertainers of any sort, and leaders. A different type of charisma is just as important to spies. In the final measure a high value for charisma means people will react to you in the way you desire. Here are some comparative values for charisma:

Charisma	Example
3	Hunchback of Notre Dame
5	An ugly used-car salesman
7	Richard Nixon today
10	Average person
12	Team coach
14	Magnum, P.I.
16	Henry Kissinger/Jim DiGriz
18	Dr. Who/Prof. Harold Hill (Centauri)

HIT POINTS

Hit points represent the total amount of damage a hero can take before he is killed or knocked out. You can receive damage from being wounded in a battle, through starvation, or even through a mental attack. Hit points measure more than just how many times the hero can be battered over the head before he is knocked out. They also represent the ability to keep striving toward a goal. A poorly paid mercenary may have only a few hit points, even though he is a hulking brute of a man, because the first time he receives even a slight wound he will withdraw from the fight. A blacksmith's apprentice who won't accept defeat will have a higher number of hit points.

A character's hit points can be lost through a wound to a specific part of the body or through general damage to the body itself. This general damage can be caused by a poison, a bad fall, or even exhaustion and starvation. Pushing your body too far beyond its limits may result in a successful action at the price of the loss of a few hit points. All these losses are treated in the same manner.

Hit points lost are subtracted from the total on the hero's record sheet. When a hero has lost all of his hit points, then that character has failed. When this happens you will be told to which section to turn. Here you will often find a description of the failure and its consequences for the hero.

The hit points for the opponents the hero meets in combat are given in the adventure. You should keep track of these hit points on a piece of scrap paper. When a monster or opponent has lost all of their hit points, they have lost the fight. If a character is fighting more than one opponent, then you should keep track of each of their hit points. Each will continue to fight until it has 0 hit points. When everyone on one side of the battle has no hit points left, the combat is over.

Even the best played character can lose all of his hit points when you roll too many bad dice during a combat. If the hero loses all of his hit points the adventure may have ended in failure. You will be told so in the next section you are instructed to turn to. In this case you can turn back to the first section and begin again. This time you will have the advantage of having learned some of the hazards the hero will face.

TAKING CHANCES

There will be occasions where you will have to decide whether the hero should attempt to perform some action which involves risk. This might be to climb a steep cliff, jump a pit, or juggle three daggers. There will be other cases where it might benefit the hero to notice something subtle or remember an ancient ballad perfectly. In all of these cases you will be asked to roll three six-sided dice (3 D6) and compare the total of all three dice to the hero's value for the appropriate ability.

For example, if the hero is attempting to juggle three balls, then for him to do so successfully you would have to roll a total equal to or less than the hero's value for dexterity. If your total was less than this dexterity value, then you would be directed to a section describing how the balls looked as they were skillfully juggled. If you rolled a higher value than that for dexterity, then you would be told to read a section which describes the embarrassment of dropping the balls, and being laughed at by the audience.

Where the decision is a judgment call, such as whether to take the left or right staircase, it is left entirely to you. Somewhere in the adventure or in the original novels there will be some piece of information which would indicate that the left staircase leads to a trap and the right to your goal. No die roll will be needed for a judgment decision.

In all cases you will be guided at the end of each section as to exactly what you need do. If you have any questions you should refer back to these rules.

MAGICAL ITEMS AND SPECIAL EQUIPMENT

There are many unusual items which appear in the pages of this adventure. When it is possible for them to be taken by the hero, you will be given the option of doing so. One or more of these items may be necessary to the successful completion of the adventure. You will be given the option of taking these at the end of a section. If you choose to pick up an item and succeed in getting it, you should list that item on the hero's record sheet. There is no guarantee that deciding to take an item means you will actually obtain it. If someone owns it already they are quite likely to resent your efforts to take it. In some cases things may not even be all they appear to be or the item may be trapped or cursed. Having it may prove a detriment rather than a benefit.

All magical items give the hero a bonus (or penalty) on certain die rolls. You will be told when this applies, and often given the option of whether or not to use the item. You will be instructed at the end of the section on how many points to add to or subtract from your die roll. If you choose to use an item which can function only once, such as a magic potion or hand grenade, then you will also be instructed to remove the item from your record sheet. Certain items, such as a magic sword, can be used many times. In this case you will be told when you obtain the item when you can apply the bonus. The bonus for a magic sword could be added every time a character is in hand-to-hand combat.

Other special items may allow a character to fly, walk through fire, summon magical warriors, or many other things. How and when they affect play will again be told to you in the paragraphs at the end of the sections where you have the choice of using them.

Those things which restore lost hit points are a

special case. You may choose to use these at any time during the adventure. If you have a magical healing potion which returns 1 D6 of lost hit points, you may add these points when you think it is best to. This can even be during a combat in the place of a round of attack. No matter how many healing items you use, a character can never have more hit points than he begins the adventure with.

There is a limit to the number of special items any character may carry. In any Crossroads™ adventure the limit is four items. If you already have four special items listed on your record sheet, then one of these must be discarded in order to take the new item. Any time you erase an item off the record sheet, whether because it was used or because you wish to add a new item, whatever is erased is permanently lost. It can never be "found" again, even if you return to the same location later in the adventure.

Except for items which restore hit points, the hero can only use an item in combat or when given the option to do so. The opportunity will be listed in the instructions.

In the case of an item which can be used in every combat, the bonus can be added or subtracted as the description of the item indicates. A +2 sword would add two points to any total rolled in combat. This bonus would be used each and every time the hero attacks. Only one attack bonus can be used at a time. Just because a hero has both a +1 and a +2 sword doesn't mean he knows how to fight with both at once. Only the better bonus would apply.

If a total of 12 is needed to hit an attacking monster and the hero has a +2 sword, then you will only need to roll a total of 10 on the three dice to successfully strike the creature.

You could also find an item, perhaps enchanted armor, which could be worn in all combat and would have the effect of subtracting its bonus from the total of any opponent's attack on its wearer. (Bad guys can wear magic armor, too.) If a monster normally would need a 13 to hit a character who has obtained a set of +2 armor, then the monster would now need a total of 15 to score a hit. An enchanted shield would operate in the same way, but could never be used when the character was using a weapon which needed both hands, such as a pike, longbow, or two-handed sword.

COMBAT

There will be many situations where the hero will be forced, or you may choose, to meet an opponent in combat. The opponents can vary from a wild beast, to a human thief, or an unearthly monster. In all cases the same steps are followed.

The hero will attack first in most combats unless you are told otherwise. This may happen when there is an ambush, other special situations, or because the opponent simply has a much higher dexterity.

At the beginning of a combat section you will be given the name or type of opponent involved. For each combat five values are given. The first of these is the total on three six-sided dice needed for the attacker to hit the hero. Next to this value is the value the hero needs to hit these opponents. After these two values is listed the hit points of the opponent. If there is more than one opponent, each one will have the same number. (See the Hit Points section included earlier if you are unclear as to what these do.) Under the value needed to be hit by the opponent is the hit points of damage that it will do to the hero when it attacks successfully. Finally, under the total needed for the hero to successfully hit an opponent is the damage he will do with the different weapons he might have. Unlike a check for completing a daring action (where you wish to roll under a value), in a combat you have to roll the value given or higher on three six-sided dice to successfully hit an opponent.

For example:
Here is how a combat between the hero armed with a sword and three brigands armed only with daggers is written:

BRIGANDS

To hit the hero: 14	*To be hit: 12*	*Hit points: 4*
Damage with	*Damage with*	
daggers: 1 D6	*sword: 2 D6*	
(used by the	(used by the hero)	
brigands)		

There are three brigands. If two are killed (taken to 0 hit points) the third will flee in panic.

If the hero wins, turn to section 85.

If he is defeated, turn to section 67.

RUNNING AWAY

Running rather than fighting, while often desirable, is not always possible. The option to run away is available only when listed in the choices. Even when this option is given, there is no guarantee the hero can get away safely.

THE COMBAT SEQUENCE

Any combat is divided into alternating rounds. In most cases the hero will attack first. Next, surviving opponents will have the chance to fight back. When both have attacked one round will have been completed. A combat can have any number of rounds and continues until the hero or his opponents are defeated. Each round is the equivalent of six seconds. During this time all the parties in the combat may actually take more than one swing at each other.

The steps in resolving a combat in which the hero attacks first are as follows:

1. Roll three six-sided dice. Total the numbers showing on all three and add any bonuses from weapons or special circumstances. If this total is the same or greater than the second value given, "to hit the opponent," then the hero has successfully attacked.

2. If the hero attacks successfully, the next step is to determine how many hit points of damage he did to the opponent. The die roll for this will be given below the "to hit opponent" information.

3. Subtract any hit points of damage done from the opponent's total.

4. If any of the enemy have one or more hit points left, then the remaining opponent or opponents now can attack. Roll three six-sided dice for each attacker. Add up each of these sets of three dice. If the total is the same or greater than the value listed after "to hit the hero" in the section describing the combat, the attack was successful.

5. For each hit roll the number of dice listed for damage. Subtract the total from the number of hit points the hero has at that time. Enter the new, lower total on the hero's record sheet.

If both the hero and one or more opponents have hit points left, the combat continues. Start again at step one. The battle ends only when the hero is killed, all the opponents are killed, or all of one side has run away. A hero cannot, except through a healing potion or spells or when specifically told to during the adventure, regain lost hit points. A number of small wounds from several opponents will kill a character as thoroughly as one titanic, unsuccessful combat with a hill giant.

DAMAGE

The combat continues, following the sequence given below, until either the hero or his opponents have no hit points. In the case of multiple opponents, subtract hit points from one opponent until the total reaches 0 or less. Extra hit points of damage done on the round when each opponent is defeated are lost. They do not carry over to the next enemy in the group. To win the combat, you must eliminate all of an opponent's hit points.

The damage done by a weapon will vary depending on who is using it. A club in the hands of a child will do far less damage than the same club wielded by a hill giant. The maximum damage is given as a number of six-sided dice. In some cases the maximum will be less than a whole die. This is abbreviated by a minus sign followed by a number. For example, D6−2, meaning one roll of a six-sided dice, minus two. The total damage can never be less than zero, meaning no damage done. 2 D6−1 means that you should roll two six-sided dice and then subtract one from the total of them both.

A combat may, because of the opponent involved, have one or more special circumstances. It may be that the enemy will surrender or flee when its hit point total falls below a certain level, or even that reinforcements will arrive to help the bad guys after so many rounds. You will be told of these special situations in the lines directly under the combat values.

Now you may turn to section 1.

NIALL

Strength: 15
Intelligence: 13
Wisdom/Luck: 12
Constitution: 14
Dexterity: 14
Charisma: 11

Hit Points: 19

Magic Items
1.
2.
3.

Items: Armor, Sword, Shield

Special Events

* **1** *

"A goblet," says Arthur, looking straight into the Irishman's eyes. "Just a goblet. A bit fancier than usual, but otherwise just another goblet." The British king turns his eyes to the tip of his sword, which he is using to draw dragons in the dust at his feet. Merlin sits at his side on one of the Roman-style dining couches drawn up to the low, inlaid table.

Across the table, Niall mac Llyr scratches his forehead for a few seconds, then asks, "But why do you want it?" At the sheer irreverence of the question, Merlin begins to get up. Arthur waves him back.

"You are an Irishman," the king replies, "and when Mael mac Ronan destroyed my dragon, I learned that I should respect Irishmen more than I had. But I learned to hate them, too, because I needed that dragon more than I can say. So don't push me, Niall mac Llyr, or you may find out where my respect stops."

Niall scrapes his boot with an oak twig and grinds his teeth. Obviously, Arthur will answer only the questions he feels like answering. Well, thinks Niall, if *Why?* has failed, and *What?* has yielded little, perhaps *How?* and *Where?* will accomplish more. *Who?*, he realizes, is either irrelevant or unknown.

"Where do I find this goblet? Do you know?" Again Merlin starts, and Niall realizes that the second part of the question probably sounded as presumptuous as the *Why?* question. But Arthur answers before Merlin moves.

"No, I don't know where to find it. If I did, I'd

Section 1

likely get it myself." He pauses and runs his fingers through his beard. "But at last you've asked a question that has some importance, Irishman. I don't know where the goblet is, but I know where it isn't. I've had my Companions looking for it for years, between wars and raiding the Saxons, and I'm damned certain that the thing isn't anywhere in my realm. The Saxons and Picts I've tortured know nothing about it at all. We know that it came west from the continent, so if it's not on this island, that leaves just one place it could be." He stops, raises his head, and again begins to stare intensely into Niall's eyes. A long minute later, he resumes.

"The goblet," he says, "is in Ireland. That's why I called you here. Mael mac Ronan refused to help me, refused to go back to Ireland. He's off in Gaul somewhere with his whore, Veleda, and that bloody Dane he never parts company with. But he told me about you, about some giant you're supposed to have killed, and about what he called your love for your homeland. I need someone who can roam freely in Ireland, and who can find things out that would be forever closed to an outsider like me."

Niall lies back on his elbows, then begins to chew on the oak twig. He hasn't expected this much candor from Arthur, who rarely explains anything to anybody, and he wonders if he can keep it going. "Even if it is in Ireland, Leader, it's going to take a while to find it. Ireland isn't as tiny as most Britons seem to think."

"True," replies Arthur. "That's why I'm giving you a year."

"Besides that," Merlin breaks in, "you know your

Section 1

way around, and you know people to talk to. "We . . ." He checks himself. "The Leader doesn't expect you to get down on your hands and knees and search every blade of grass. He wants you to use your wits to find out where the goblet is, then get it and bring it to him. Pretty simple, I would think."

"Yes," Niall says. "Pretty simple." What do these Britons think Ireland is? he thinks to himself. A few scattered huts peopled with old, gullible fools? If that's the case, why hasn't Arthur just walked in and taken it? They can fight, these Irishmen, and they are mysterious besides. I may be one of them, but even I don't understand half their mysteries, half their legends, half their beliefs. Once you leave, even if only for a year, much of the land becomes hidden from you forever. You can't get it back.

"Still," Arthur goes on, "we haven't given you much to go on. I've asked you to find my goblet, or at least what will be my goblet once I have it, but I haven't told you what it looks like. Partly . . ." He paused. "Partly . . . it's because I don't really know what it looks like. Nobody does. Nobody's seen it for . . . well, over five centuries. But it's even older than that, and that's the best clue I can give you. The goblet you want is probably eight centuries old, maybe more." Niall tries to calculate how many eight hundred-year-old goblets there must be in Ireland, artifacts and utensils left over from the Celtic tribes, and figures there must be hundreds. Arthur continues, "But this goblet has other features, too. It's fairly tall, almost a foot high. Apparently, it's pure gold with no decoration on the outside, not even on the stem. Its only ornamentation is on the inside. If you look into the goblet, at the bottom you will see a tiny ruby. That's all I know about it."

"It's a help," says Niall. "I'm sure the old tribes left many goblets scattered throughout Ireland, but the one you've described is quite different. No self-respecting Celt would fashion a plain gold goblet. The kings decorated their goldware with battle scenes, and the Druids engraved sacrificial emblems or tall oaks on their chalices and plates."

Merlin, his old robe wrapped loosely about him, has begun to fidget by this time, but Arthur doesn't seem to notice. Niall looks at Merlin, and the wizard nods once, then closes his eyes. Arthur is drawing something in the dust.

"Here," says the king. "Here is as close as I can get to what I think the goblet looks like. It has a tall, slim cup and a fairly short stem. The base is round but not very big. There are probably no handles." He looks piercingly at Niall. "Any more questions?"

Niall stares at the drawing, then shakes his head. "No," he says. "I'll start tomorrow."

"Fine," Arthur replies. "I'll have supplies prepared for you." Niall nods, then rises and leaves the tent.

Outside, the wind has stopped. For days it has torn at the trees and blown the late August dust all through the camp, so that everything—even the fresh meat and the water—feels like sand. Several tents are uprooted every day, and one of the soldier's wives has been lost in the storm. Even Arthur's famous training maneuvers, which he holds every day even during lulls in battle, have stopped, because the king fears injury to the horses. Not that Arthur makes it seem

Section 1

like a holiday. His men spend the days cleaning, washing and dusting everything in sight, putting up barriers against the wind, and bringing in water from the river over a mile away. By the end of the second day, most of the men wished they could go back to training.

As he walks, Niall laughs at his memory of the Companions helping with the cleaning. Lancelot, especially, objected to the work, declaring for all to hear that a Companion is trained for war, not for householding. When the complaints reached the Leader's ears, Arthur simply gave him tasks even more tedious than cleaning. Nor are the other Companions any happier, although they don't express themselves as openly as Lancelot. Only Arthur's seneschal, Cei, as private as always, carries out his new jobs without complaining. What the rest of Arthur's army is doing—the rest of Britons and those warriors less loyal than the Companions—Niall has been unable to find out, but he doubts they are scrubbing down the horses. Out looking for women, more likely, he thinks, the ones who somehow get temporarily lost in the blanket of dust.

Lancelot appears suddenly out of the storm, and Niall nearly walks into him. The Companion grabs the Irishman's left arm and squints at him through the blowing dust. "Irishman," he says, "I want to talk to you." His voice is controlled, but it is not calm.

"Can it wait?"

"No."

Niall shrugs. "Then talk."

"No, not here." Lancelot looks around nervously, then motions towards the Irishman's tent. Niall had hoped this wouldn't happen. Lancelot was not easy to get rid of, but Niall nods and leads the way into his tent.

Like all the tents in Arthur's camp, Niall's is small and nearly empty. A thin blanket serves as his bed, a pack as his pillow. An old bucket in the corner holds water, which Niall himself has collected from the river. Piled in the opposite corner, under a threadbare old coverlet, is Niall's equipment: an unremarkable sword, a less remarkable wooden shield, and a set of armor, fashioned of boiled leather. The Irishman doesn't even bother to guard his meager belongings.

"I know I'm supposed to offer you something, to prove I'm a good host," Niall says. "But, as you see, there's nothing here. I'd take on the whole Saxon army for a beer, but that stuff seemed to disappear as soon as the dust started. I won't ask who got it all."

"I don't know," Lancelot replies. "I don't drink it. I'm usually on duty."

Niall smiles. He's heard of Lancelot's drunken binges, that he can take no more than three glasses of beer before tearing the camp apart. That's probably why he keeps himself on duty most of the time, Niall thinks. "Anyway," he asks, "what do you want?"

"Among other things, your head, Irishman, and the heads of Mael mac Ronan and Starkad the Dane for making a fool of me, and the heads of the entire Saxon army. That would do to start. But right now it's the 'among other things' that matter, because if I take your head the Leader would take mine. I'll just ask you one question. What does he want you to do?"

"A job," says Niall, then waits for the silence to end.

"What kind of job?"

Section 1

"One that will take me away for a while, but then will bring me back." Niall pauses, keeping his eyes on the Companion. Lancelot, he realizes, is going to keep pressing for more information.

"I see," Lancelot says, "you're not going to tell me. Not willingly, at least."

Niall nods. "I doubt your Leader would want me to. If he wanted you to know, I figure he'd tell you."

Lancelot stares at the tent's entrance. "I could force you to tell me," he mumbles, "but that wouldn't do any good. You'd just run to Arthur, so I'll make you an offer." He pauses. "Tell me what your job is, and I'll give you any piece of my equipment you want. Tell me all the details, and I'll give you two."

Niall looks hard at the Companion, watching for further signs. There is something wrong with the offer. At first he thought Lancelot was merely curious, or jealous because Arthur has chosen an outsider for an important task. But now he sees there is more to Lancelot's questioning than mere curiosity. To offer his equipment—his sword that was rumored to be magical, his superb gauntlets, his precious lance—is simply unlike the greedy, selfish Lancelot he has come to know. Perhaps it is just this change that convinces Niall of what to do, or maybe it is Lancelot's obsessive hatred of everyone who is not a Companion and of the Irish in particular. Or maybe the dust, which has begun to fray even the best-kept tempers, has finally gotten to him. Whatever the reason, Niall stands up, stares down at the seated Companion, and says, "Lancelot, get out of this tent before I drive my fist down your throat."

Lancelot rises. "I've offered everything I can, Irishman," he snarls, "and I don't like to be refused. Now I'll offer the reward I wanted to give you in the first place." He steps once towards Niall and holds out his arm. The Irishman clasps it in the manner of a Roman handshake and begins to twist. The Companion does the same, and the two men wait to see whose strength will wither first, knowing that the arm that loses will snap at the elbow. The wind rises to a howl outside, and the dust seeps in endlessly, through the entrance and under the walls. Straining but motionless, Lancelot and Niall stare at each other as the dust settles on their faces and into their eyes.

Long minutes pass. The strain grows. Niall feels himself weakening, feels his grasp on the Companion's arm working itself loose, feels his opponent's rage overtaking Niall's own determination. He wonders if Lancelot feels the same, or if he remains as strong as his hate-filled stare. The Irishman sees the dust swirling through the room, and in his strain he thinks he can feel each tiny grain strike his face and fall on his arms. Throbbing, his eyes begin to lose focus. All his concentration is bound up in his arm, in trying to stop it from turning. Suddenly, with his heart pounding in his temples, he feels his arm start to yield. It turns ever so slightly, a fraction of an inch, yet Niall cannot stop it. With one last groaning effort, the Irishman blacks out.

He wakes to the sight of a white beard only inches from his face. Merlin the wizard bends over him, his lips moving soundlessly and his hand tracing the wrinkles on Niall's forehead. In an effort to jump away from the old man's huge face, Niall cracks his head on the floor and cries out.

Section 1

"Oh, hello," Merlin says. "I thought you'd never wake up."

Niall almost hisses. "What are you doing? And where's Lancelot?"

"Second question first. Lancelot is lying asleep in his own tent. I'm cleaning the dust from your face."

Niall continues his questioning. "That's not exactly what I meant. Why isn't Lancelot here? And why are you here? And why do you care about my face?" Suddenly Niall realizes that he is gesticulating with his right arm. "And why isn't my arm broken?" His questions are practically screams.

"Oh, calm down," says a smiling Merlin. "I can't answer all these questions at once. First of all, your arm isn't broken because I stopped the duel you and that stupid Companion were having. It would have done neither of you any good, and it might have ruined Arthur's plans. Next, I'm here because I want to talk to you. I thought you realized that when I nodded to you in Arthur's tent. Last, I don't care about your face. But I do care about the wrinkles on your forehead. They're getting deeper."

"So what?" Once again, Niall has received far more explanation than he'd figured on, so he thinks he'll try to keep it going.

Merlin's eyes narrow. "This dust is having an unusual effect on everybody except perhaps me. Several of you seem to be visibly aging, you and Arthur most noticeably so, and other people are growing more impatient as the days pass."

Niall shakes his head. "That's hardly unusual, wizard. This storm's enough to make anybody hate the world."

"True," replies the wizard. "But there's more to it

than that. I've seen days on end of cold, rainy weather that irritated everyone, and I've seen spells of intense heat that had people ready to kill whatever moved. I've seen other dust storms, too. You may not believe it, but there's more to the land of the Britons than just sogginess. But this one . . . well, this one's different. I'd like to know why."

"And that's what you want to talk to me about?" Niall asks.

"No, but it might be related to what I have to say to you." He stops. "Give me a minute, though. I want to get some water." He leaves the tent, and Niall lies back on the pillow Merlin has fashioned from the blanket. His head throbs, but he is wide awake.

"This won't take long," Merlin says after Niall has downed nearly a pail of water and half a loaf of bread. "As you've no doubt guessed by now, I'm worried. Oh, some say I worry too much—Arthur is one of them—but I never worry needlessly. When I worry, there's always something to worry about, even if that something isn't apparent for quite some time. Well, I'm worried now, more than I have been for a long while."

He pauses for rhetorical effect, then continues. "This dust storm is unnatural. Maybe even supernatural. Yes, we get dust storms. I've already said that. But they don't carry on like this, and they don't have this effect on people. Dust storms are a nuisance, a hindrance to Arthur's plans, but that's all. He gets upset, and that makes everyone upset, but life goes on pretty well unaltered.

"This storm is different, though. I've thought that ever since it started, though Arthur didn't want to hear about it. He's still working on a way to repay Mael mac Ronan for destroying his wyvern, *my* wyvern I should say, and he hasn't been very receptive lately. Nevertheless, I've worked at this dust for hours, almost without stop for the past three days, and I believe I've come up with at least one of the answers I sought. It's not an answer I like."

Niall listens, wondering why Merlin is confiding in him, but the wizard barely pauses.

"Arthur doesn't know it, but that goblet he's sending you after has something to do with it. Not with the dust storm, not directly at least. The storm itself is natural enough. What's unnatural is the dust." He scoops up a handful from the dirt floor. Then, tearing off a small piece of his battered robe, he pours a trickle of dust into the cloth and looks at Niall. "Watch this closely," he says, and holds the cloth up to Niall's eyes.

Niall watches. Nothing seems to happen. "I don't understand," he says.

"Look," says Merlini. "Look very closely at the dust. Watch what it does to the cloth."

Again Niall watches, this time for a full minute. Suddenly he sees what Merlin means. The dust settles on the cloth and slowly, very slowly, begins to sink into it. "It's eating through," he whispers.

"Yes. But keep watching. Watch one of the grains of dust that has eaten its way into the cloth."

Staring at the dust, even though the concentration hurts his already pain-wracked head, Niall at first sees nothing. But as he continues to stare, something begins to happen to the dust particles. They begin to change color, from light brown to a darker brown and then, unexpectedly, to a dark red, a red beyond the color of blood. Niall shakes his head to clear it, then looks again. Yes, they are red, and the cloth where they gather is turning red with them.

"How can that be?" he askes the wizard.

"Sorcery," Merlin replies. "Witchcraft, wizardry —call it what you will. Somehow the dust is enchanted, perhaps cursed. When you fall asleep at night, a thin film of it covers you like a blanket, and throughout the night it starts eating through your skin, just as it ate through my robe. More slowly, of course; skin is stronger and less porous than the cheap cloth used in this part of the world. But over the course of days, it will eat through completely."

Niall breaks in. "But how long does it take? And what happens when it does?"

"Yes. Those are the right questions. I've been thinking of them for the last thirty hours or so. And for the first while I didn't have any idea how to get the answers.

"But suddenly I began to think about Arthur's goblet. He's been wanting that goblet for two years, ever since he heard about it, because he thinks it is magical, perhaps as a replacement for his dragon, perhaps just an artifact he thinks will help his image. But when I sat and remembered what I had read long ago about this goblet, I remembered that it has a ruby in the bottom of its cup. Suddenly I felt—*knew*, maybe—that the dust and the goblet were somehow related."

At Merlin's pause, Niall feels nothing but confusion. He is still completely ignorant of the importance of the goblet, except that Arthut wants it enough to risk asking a stranger's help (which might just as easily mean that he thinks it impossible to procure). Now Merlin is asking him to see its relationship to a magical dust he doesn't understand at all. He's always heard that Merlin speaks in riddles, and now he knows it to be true, despite the seeming ease of the wizard's explanations of the dust itself. Unlike everyone around him, Merlin is able to take disparate facts and synthesize them to form valid conclusions; he understands logic. For the Companions, for Niall and apparently even for Arthur, intelligence is measured in degrees of common sense, not logic. For Merlin, it is the other way around. Merlin does not really speak in riddles, but he also seldom relies on common sense. Those who listen become quickly perplexed.

To his credit, Niall now realizes this about Merlin, but the knowledge does little to help him relate the reddening dust to the ruby in the goblet. While he thinks, he feels Merlin looking at him, sizing him up, making a decision about him. Then, at once, it seems to Niall that Merlin is urging him on, coaxing him towards an answer. Idea after idea swirl through his brain as the grains of dust have swirled through his tent, repelling each other, utterly refusing to cooperate. But then, a will beyond his own begins drawing the ideas towards one another, forcing them, despite their desperate independence, to work as one. Niall's brain aches with the pain of thinking beyond his intelligence. His mouth opens in a soundless "NO!"

Suddenly, the pain stops. Niall opens his eyes and looks at the wizard. Obviously drained, seeming years older than a moment before, Merlin sits motionless, his head hung on his chest. Niall places his left hand under the old man's chin and raises the eyes to meet his own. Merlin's eyes are half-closed, but still full of questions.

Niall says, slowly and softly, "I understand." Merlin almost smiles.

"Tell me, Irishman. Tell me what you understand." For over an hour, Merlin had slept so deeply that Niall checked repeatedly to see if he still had a pulse. Now he is awake but still clearly exhausted.

Niall thinks for a minute before speaking. "The dust storm is unnatural. You told me that. But now I see how it is unnatural. No, wait," he says as Merlin tries to interrupt, "let me try this. It's important that I know how to explain it." Merlin nods.

"Let me start with the goblet. It's made of unadorned gold, with a ruby deep in the drinking cup. The ruby's attached, which means it won't move, even if you tip the goblet to drink out of it. When light hits the ruby, any clear liquid in the goblet looks red. The pure gold helps this effect because it reflects light well. Am I right so far?" Merlin continues to stare at Niall but gives no response.

"Let me go on. Red liquid—blood, obviously. And wine, too. Not real blood or real wine, but liquid that looks like blood and wine. Reminds you of blood and wine. I'm not putting it very well."

Merlin breaks in. "Symbolizes blood and wine. Try 'symbolizes.'"

"Okay, symbolizes. And blood and wine have something to do with the reason Arthur wants the goblet. Right?"

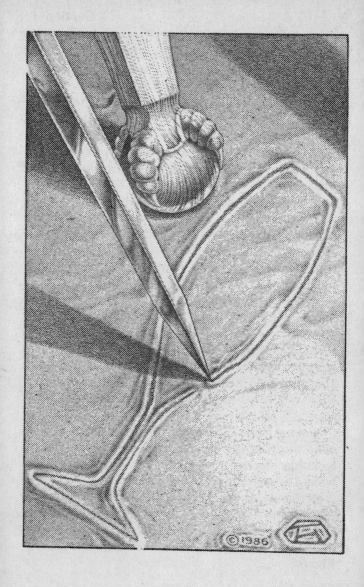

"Yes," says Merlin. "But go on with the other for now."

Niall waits in thought, then continues. "You think there's a relationship between the ruby and the blood in the goblet, and the dust in this damned dust storm." He wipes the grit from his face. "The goblet is meant to be drunk from, which means you turn it over, upside down. As soon as you do that, the ruby is on top, the goblet is empty, the red liquid is gone."

He pauses. "I understand, and I really think I do, but I'm stumped here. How do I explain the rest?" He then falls silent for several minutes.

The old wizard begins speaking slowly, almost in a chant. "Arthur wants the goblet because it has long been lost. More seriously, it has long been unused. And an unused goblet, if it is not properly protected, gathers dust, just like any other cup that is not frequently washed. Dust soils. It makes things unclean, impure. And if the grains of dust are tiny enough, and the covering is thin enough, and light shines in the goblet, the ruby will catch the light and send it back red, as always. But this time the goblet will contain not red liquid but rather red dust. Red dirt. Impure red. If somebody—or something—turns the goblet upside down, what spills out is the same, impure, red dust. The red ruby will shine down from above it.

"No human being, Niall mac Llyr, has drunk from this goblet for many years, perhaps many centuries. Once it contained wine—blood if you believe all the stories—and this wine symbolized life and death at the same time. The death of one man, but the life of everyone else. Replace the wine with dust, though, and you get rid of the 'life' half of the symbol. The dust that pours from the goblet is the symbol only of death."

Niall waits for Merlin to continue, but the wizard has plainly stopped. Raising his eyes to meet the old man's, the Irishman says, "And this dust that falls on us is, somehow, the same dust that falls from Arthur's golden goblet. This storm brings the dust of death."

"Yes," said Merlin. "That is what I fear."

"I thought so," Niall replies, and shakes his head. "But how can that be, wizard? How can the dust from one little cup be covering all these men, all this earth, maybe this entire island? How can that be possible?"

Merlin sits in silence for a long time. Staring at the sheets of fine dust that have swirled through the entrance, Niall waits for no answer, patient only because he has no choice. But no matter how long the silence lasts, how unholy the sight of the dust and the howl of the storm, when the old man finally speaks, Niall wishes he had never heard the answer.

"I don't know," says Merlin. "That's what you have to find out." With that he rises, shakes out his robe and goes out of the tent, leaving Niall alone with his terror.

Sleepless, Niall passes what remains of the night deep in thought and fear. Until now, his only contact with the supernatural has been a Pictish witch who brought to life the statue of an ancient king, but the statue had simply taken one step and fallen in ruins. The blood-dust is far different. It is at once more real and more fantastic. Niall is not forced, as he was with the statue that almost stepped on him, to believe in it at all. If he chooses not to, he can simply find Arthur's goblet and either return it or keep it for his own. His problems are great only if he decides to believe.

As if sensing the Irishman's wavering convictions, Merlin enters the tent just as the dawn is about to appear. "Come with me," he says, and leaves the tent once again. Niall gets up, fixes his knife through his belt and goes outside into the storm. Merlin stands beside a pale gray horse, feeding him grass and talking into his ear. At Niall's approach, the horse snorts and Merlin stops what he is doing.

"You must go now," says the wizard, as the horse nuzzles his arm. "There is no more time."

"Now?" Niall almost shouts. "But what about supplies? Food? Money? By the god to whom my people swear, I've hardly even slept." A sudden swirl of dust blinds him as his anger grows.

"I can't help that," Merlin says calmly. "I've received a visitor this night, and she has shown me the need for haste. Here is a horse and two large sacks filled with such food and drink as I could gather. The horse is called Anwyn: he's a good horse. I've managed to pack a little beer."

Niall sees through the wizard's calm. Merlin is tense, maybe even scared, and his efforts at control are about to disintegrate. But Niall continues his questions.

"A visitor? She?" He waits for an answer.

"Yes, a visitor. A vision, more like, even though I don't really believe in visions. I practice sorcery, Irishman, but I know what sorcery is and I can control it. I can't control spirits that wander around becoming visions, can I? They frighten me because I don't know what to do with them. I never have."

"You've had visions before?"

"Of course. All good magicians have. Usually they come from demons, though."

"What was this one?"

"Not a demon." Merlin pales. "This one was . . . well, a goddess, if I'm not mistaken."

Niall's eyes open wide, but he quickly brings himself back under control. "Hold on now," he says. "A goddess? But you don't believe . . ."

"True," says Merlin. "But neither do I deny. Yes, the Christians have convinced me—and most of us—that the old gods and goddesses are false deities, and that Christ is the only son of the true God, but that doesn't stop the others from existing. Deities don't come and go, Irishman: only their worshippers do. But all this is beside the point. I said I was visited by a goddess, but it was a strange vision, unclear and not at all comforting. It took me over an hour, after she left, to interpret her words. That's the problem with visions. It takes a great education merely to understand them, but I'm sure now that I know."

A pause, then Merlin continues. "She showed me the goblet, Niall, and it was indeed turned upside down, just as I had thought. But I couldn't see it properly, almost as if a cloud of dust—red dust, yes—obscured my sight. But under the goblet was a dead man, the symbol that we too are being buried. At first I could not recognize him. Finally I did, though, and then I understood. The dead man was Uther Pendragon. Do you know the name?"

"Arthur's father, wasn't he?"

"Yes, although some say otherwise. But he was indeed Arthur's father, for I helped him enter the bed of Igraine, Arthur's mother. Still, that's unimportant. Two things matter, as far as I can tell. Uther, to many of his followers, was a god. That makes Arthur a deity as well, if you follow the logic. To them, Uther's death meant the end of his godhood, because the Britons, unlike the Irish and the Druids, won't accept a dead god. Their gods must live on, which is why Christ became so important to them." He pauses.

Niall thinks for a moment, then breaks the silence, "If Uther really was a god, and if Arthur is a deity as well, and if that's proven, what happens to the followers of Christ?"

"Precisely," says the wizard. "That's the exact question. I don't know the answer. But the other thing that matters here is that the goblet is clearly connected to Uther's death, or burial, or godhood, or something, and that's where you come in. Find the goblet, and bring it back here."

Puzzled, Niall asks, "Why?"

"I don't know. Neither did the goddess."

"This is ridiculous," Niall replies. "What am I supposed to do with it?"

"As I said, we don't know," says the wizard. "But one person does, or at least that's what I got from the vision. One person only. Before you begin your search for the goblet, you must make one visit. On the plains of Salisbury, to our southwest, are the standing stones of the Druids. There, it is said, is Uther's grave. Find it, and he will speak to you. Uther Pendragon knows what to do."

Turn to section 2.

* **2** *

"Dried beef, dried fruit, dried bread, dried biscuits, likely even drier beer, judging from the looks of things." Niall closes the leather sack and scans the ground, southward from the road and across the plain. "And for you, Anwyn, good and faithful horse, dried grass." The horse snorts, though whether in agreement or disgust Niall cannot tell. Anwyn lowers his head to graze, but raises it with nothing to chew. He snorts again.

"Well, let me check Merlin's other sack," says the traveler, walking around in front of the horse to the other side. He loosens the ties, lifts the flap, and peers inside. "More dried food, it looks like. And a knife, though not good enough to kill anyone with. Oh, and a little bag of oats." He holds it up to Anwyn's mouth. "I don't know who Merlin put these in here for, horse, but you might as well eat them. I never could stand them."

At the bottom of the sack is an old blanket, rolled up to fit a fairly small space. Niall draws it out, lays it on the gound, and unwraps it. From it falls, to his immense delight, a wine flagon. Old, to be sure, and off color, but if it isn't empty at least it does not leak. Opening it, he puts his nose to the spout and smells.

"By the gods to whom my people pray!" he shouts. "He did pack some beer!" The Irishman raises the flagon to his lips and fills his thirsty mouth, swishing it around to savor the taste. Beer! he thinks. Not only something to drink, but the best drink possible. But suddenly his mouth puckers, his eyebrows furl and his eyes close as he tastes in the beer the grit that sweeps through Arthur's camp and gets into everything. He spits his drink as far as he can.

"Dust," he snarls. "Dust in every damned thing I own." The dust storm itself he has left behind, only hours after leaving Arthur's camp, but all his equipment and all his food still remind him, as does the parched land around him, of his hatred of the wind and the dirt that would not stop. During his ride, he has seen more reminders: dried-up creek beds, grain crops standing dead in the fields, gnarled apples on withered grass beneath the trees. Only in the last few hours has he seen any change; the grass seems to be getting greener.

The old Roman road that runs westward from Londinium is not arduous, but it is certainly boring. Once out of Arthur's camp and moving away from the channel and rivers that run into it, Niall had seen the hills flatten out and the fields open wide. Soon even the forests disappeared. During most of the first day, Niall had fought through the clouds of dust, but early this morning the wind had stopped and the dust was visible only behind him. But the dust, Niall could tell, had moved in from the west, and the road had been dry and filthy. Then, finally out of the storm and beyond the dust's enormous reach, Niall had watched the land rolling gently southward and flat to the north. Of all Arthur's lands, he had thought, this must be the worst.

Now, at dusk of the second day, Niall sees green in the grass to the south, and he smiles. "Come, Anwyn," he says to his horse. "Let's get off the road.

Section 2

We have to go south anyway, and even though the road would take us very close to the Druidstones, following it too far might be dangerous. I'd rather approach the stones from the fields."

He leads Anwyn a mile south from the Roman road, then crouches down and touches the grass. "It's wet!" he exclaims, and guides Anwyn's head down to it. A minute later, when he wants to resume the march, the horse shakes his head and refuses to move, refuses even to lift his mouth from the grass. "Okay," says Niall, "you stay here. You've earned it. I'll go a bit further by myself, then come back for you. You won't be as hungry by then."

Niall walks southward across the plain toward the small, rolling hills not far away. With the light of the sun disappearing completely, he walks for a half hour, then climbs atop the first hill and looks about him. To the east it is dark, and he can see nothing. To the south, the next line of hills, larger than this first group, stands silhouetted against the blackening sky. To the west, the plain stretches out flat and uninviting.

And then, rising over the tall hills in the dusk of the southwest, Niall sees a deep blue glow. Where it comes from he does not know, but as he watches the glow brightens to a sea-blue, then a lighter, brilliant blur, and then into a green that brings to him a yearning for his home. The green yields to gold, and the gold to white, and then the white to pink darkening through crimson to a final flash of red the color of blood. And then there is only black, as the twilight fails and the moon begins its climb into the night sky.

Suddenly, still looking toward the southwest, the

Irishman spots a small fire, almost hidden, in the valley just over the next hill. Squinting, he thinks he can see a human figure, maybe two, huddled around it. Somewhere beyond those hills, he knows, is the river that runs almost straight south to the sea, and somewhere too is the source of the uncanny glow that has just lit up the night. It is now dark, and he can take the figures by surprise. Niall starts toward the fire.

But then he stops and looks behind him to his horse. The traveler can barely make out Anwyn's silhouette on the horizon, but he is there. Still, if Niall heads toward the fire, he has no guarantee that Anwyn will not wander off. Niall does not know how well he was trained. But if he returns for the horse, whoever made the fire might disappear into the night. Even if the strangers remain by the fire Anwyn will make stealth almost impossible. Undecided, Niall waits on the hill.

If Niall returns for Anwyn, turn to section 9.

If he heads for the fire, turn to section 6.

* **3** *

His sleep is sound, but his dreams are frightening. In one dream, the glow of many colors reappears in the southwest night sky, but now the colors coalesce to form the haunting image of a beautiful, black-haired woman impaled on the point of an enormous stone sword. In another dream, a black bear stumbles towards him, and he cannot move. The bear slashes at him, and when the Irishman falls the animal grasps Niall's neck and lifts him into the air. As soon as this scene fades, a third appears. Riding out of the mists of dawn comes the specter of Uther Pendragon wearing Arthur's famous helm which bears the portrait of a dragon, and carrying Pridwen, his shield, and Caliburn, his sword. Straight toward Niall he rides. At the last moment he raises Caliburn above his head and cries, "Welcome, Death. Welcome and wait. I follow now, I follow you home." And then he sweeps Caliburn wide in the air and slices off his own head, and the head of Uther Pendragon falls onto the chest of Niall mac Llyr.

The Irishman wakens with a scream.

"I told you he'd wake up, you damned fool!" shouts a black-bearded, stocky man racing toward him, a foot-long knife in his right hand glinting in the moonlight. His reflexes reacting before his sleep-befuddled brain, Niall's left hand grasps the leather sheath at his side. Then, with the man almost upon him, he rolls to his left, clasping the sheath with his left hand and grabbing hold of his wooden shield with his right. Yelling, the black-bearded man runs right past the spot where Niall had been, then loses his balance and falls on his face. Niall leaps to his feet, slings his shield over his left arm, and draws out his sword just in time to see the second man, taller than the first and red-bearded, running at him with a long sword in his right hand and a gleaming shield on his arm. Redbeard halts in front of him, and the two eye one another, each waiting for the first chance to strike.

Use the combat rules to determine who wins the fight.
Niall and Redbeard fight for three rounds before Black-
beard joins in.

REDBEARD
To hit: 10   To be hit: 9   Hit points: 12
Damage with sword: 1 D6+3

BLACKBEARD
To hit Niall: 9   To be hit: 8   Hit points: 10
Damage with knife: 1 D6

If Niall wins, turn to section 12.

If he loses, turn to section 90.

* **4** *

With the smaller man out of the way, Niall faces the
fair-haired, knife-wielding bandit.

"Who are you?" growls Lightbeard.

"You won't know me," Niall replies. "So why
bother asking?"

"What do you want?"

"Your sword, and your shield, and your rabbit. Will
you give them to me?"

Lightbeard laughs, but the sound is neither friendly nor generous.

"Then fight for them," Niall yells, and charges his
foe.

The bearded man fights well, but Niall has the edge
of experience. He was a skilled fighter before he met
the Companions, and several days of watching and
training with them has honed his skill considerably.

He dances away from Lightbeard's knife thrusts,

waiting for the one opening he needs to make this fight short. The only way he can lose, he knows, is to strike too soon, to give the advantage to his opponent.

Lightbeard grows frustrated. Slash after slash of his knife miss the quick-reflexed Irishman. Cunningly he slows his movements, but Niall knows it is merely a trick. He is ready when Lightbeard makes his move.

Both men are breathing shallowly and taking a moment to rest when Lightbeard suddenly attacks. He leaps at Niall, his knife aimed for the throat. It is the move Niall has been waiting for. He steps to his left, extending his right arm and the sword into his opponent's path. A second later, Lightbeard has impaled himself on it.

"You were quick," Niall says to the corpse, "but not quick enough."

As he stoops to wipe the sword on the bandit's tunic, Niall hears a noise behind him. Rising and turning in one motion, he sees the smaller man charging toward him. Niall ducks just in time, but the knife gashes his arm. It hurts like hell, but he has no time to be concerned about pain.

Darkbeard turns and charges again. *What an ass!* Niall thinks. *How often does he think he can get away with this? Well, what's good for one is good for the other.* The Irishman aims his sword in his foe's path and waits for the easy victory.

But Darkbeard surprises him. Ten feet from the Irishman he stops, aims his knife, and throws it. Niall raises his sword only by reflex and manages to deflect the knife. *The gods must have been watching,* he thinks to himself.

Now Darkbeard dives for his friend's knife, but Niall moves too quickly for him. One swing and Darkbeard's head rolls several feet down the hill. The Irishman drops his bloody blade next to the grisly corpse and walks to the gleaming sword.

Niall fits the sheath around his waist and slips the sword into it. Searching the bodies, he discovers nothing that will be of use. He is hungry now, but cannot linger to eat. He wraps the roasted rabbit in a small cloth sack he finds among the men's possessions. Taking up the intricately designed sheild, he throws his own into the fire where it slowly starts to burn.

With one last glance at the fight scene and then at the star-filled sky, the Irishman begins to walk back toward the waiting Anwyn.

With the sword, Niall does 1 D6+3 points of damage. The shield decreases an enemy's To Hit number by 1. Be sure to note these changes on your character record sheet.

Turn to section 11.

* **5** *

His sword drawn and shield raised, the Irishman sprints down the hill toward the fire. Darkbeard, asleep, lies between Niall and the watchman. Seeing his attacker approach, Lightbeard shifts his knife to his left hand and starts to move toward the sword that lies on the ground about twenty yards away. Niall is almost upon the sleeping man, but decides to take on

Section 6

Lightbeard first. To avoid any unexpected interference from Darkbeard, Niall aims a kick to his temple as he runs past. The sleeping man never awakens before falling into a deeper unconsciousness.

Use the combat rules to determine the outcome of this fight. Because of Niall's speed, Lightbeard is not able to reach his sword and is forced to use his knife.

If Niall defeats Lightbeard, Darkbeard awakens to carry on the fight. He attacks with his knife only, as he is untrained with the sword.

LIGHTBEARD
To hit Niall: 10 (12)   To be hit: 9   Hit points: 12
Damage with knife: 1 D6

DARKBEARD
To hit Niall: 9   To be hit: 8   Hit points: 10
Damage with knife: 1 D6

If Niall wins, turn to section 4.

If he loses, turn to section 89.

* 6 *

Running bent at the waist, Niall crosses the quarter mile to the grassy hill. Carefully and quietly, he climbs it, dropping to his knees and crawling as he nears the top.

Make a Wisdom roll.

If this roll is successful, turn to section 7.

If the roll fails, turn to section 8.

* **7** *

As he crawls ever nearer the crest of the hill, Niall's hand lands on a stone. Picking it up, he runs his fingers over it and feels that one side is perfectly smooth. Then he runs his hand over the other side and feels a pattern of lines carved into the stone's face. In an attempt to see the lines, the Irishman holds the stone above his head and tries to catch the still weak moonlight. For several seconds he squints at it, rotating it this way and that, but he can see nothing.

Then, suddenly, the moonlight seems to increase, and the lines in the stone begin to glow a dull red. They show the outline of an animal—a bear, Niall thinks, but he cannot see it well—standing on its hind legs. In the bear's paws is a skull—human or animal, Niall can't make out. When a cloud passes in front of the moon, the lines disappear.

If Niall keeps the stone, turn to section 10.

If he does not, turn to section 8.

* 8 *

Flat on the ground, barely peering over the crest of the hill, Niall looks through the dew-spotted grass toward the fire. Two men sit talking on opposite sides of the fire. They are burly but not tall. They hold knives, which they are using to eat what looks like a roasted rabbit. To the hungry Niall, the welcome smell alone is enough to make him charge the site, but something else catches his eye. Moonlight gleams off the polished blade of a large sword that lies on the ground beside the taller of the two men. Beside the sword, if Niall's sight is true, is a small metal shield. I don't know how good the equipment is, he thinks to himself, but they're a damned notion better than the old junk I'm carrying. Besides, he rationalizes, I can always sell them later.

Slowly, Niall drags himself closer to the fire, to hear what the men are saying. They sport beards, he sees now, a dark one on the shorter man and a lighter one, perhaps red, on the other. They are tired, that is clear, but they eat like men who have not long been without food. They eat, too, with more refinement than Niall expected, almost like Arthur's Companions at one of their stupid feasts. They aren't Saxons, then, and they aren't Irishmen, who Niall knows have no sense of decorum whatsoever. Britons then, but from where and on what business? He strains to hear their mumbled conversation.

"No, I don't think so," says Darkbeard. I think we should stay off the road. Otherwise we'll be targets."

Lightbeard laughs. "Targets for what, coward? We

don't even know if there's anyone on the road. We're just supposed to patrol it for a few days to find out. If we find someone, we don't even have to fight. All we have to do is report."

"True. But if we take to the road, we might not live long enough to report. Why not just stay off it, hidden in the hills? Then we're sure of getting away to make the report."

"But what about us, my friend?" Lightbeard asks. "There's no point in us going back with nothing to show for this. If we meet someone on the road, we can rob him first, then we can make the report. Who'll know?"

Darkbeard shakes his head. "I still don't like it. But right now, I'm going to get some sleep. You keep watch for a while, and if you see a traveler you can rob him to your heart's content. Wake me when you can't stay awake."

When Darkbeard lays his head down in the grass, his companion gets to his feet and begins to walk in aimless circles. After several minutes, the shorter man is obviously asleep, and Niall knows that he should attack now if he is to attack at all.

If Niall attacks, turn to section 5.

If he turns away and returns to Anwyn, turn to section 9.

* 9 *

When Niall returns to Anwyn, the horse is still grazing, although a hundred yards or so south of where he began. Anwyn whinnies softly at Niall's approach, then shakes an insect from his neck and grazes once more. Niall surveys the plain, gently rolling in the moonlight, and decides that this is as good a place as any to rest for the night. After removing Anwyn's saddle, whose square, featureless design looks more like that of a Roman of the past century than of the horse soldiers of Arthur's army, he sets Merlin's sacks on the ground beside his sword and shield. Then, the Irishman eats his dried food and washes his mouth with the gritty beer from the wine flagon, lays his head on the saddle and falls asleep.

Turn to section 3.

* 10 *

Mark an "S" in the Special Events box of Niall's character record.

The stone is valuable to Niall, but its moonlit outline, he feels, is ominous. The lines disappear in the daylight, so he is never certain what the animal is or what the skull represents. Furthermore, the stone seems to change weight, at times heavy and uncomfortable, at other times practically unnoticeable. For now, however, the stone increases his Strength by 1, and his Intelligence by 2, until otherwise directed.

Turn to section 8.

* **11** *

The next day's ride does much to revive Niall. The sun had shone hotly in the morning, but by mid-afternoon dark clouds had brought cooler air and the smell of rain. Now, with dusk approaching, Niall feels the first drops, and he looks to the sky with an intense eagerness. Even Anwyn, he thinks, seems excited by the prospect of the first rainfall in three weeks, the first chance to wash themselves of the red dust of Arthur's camp.

At the crest of the tall green hill, Niall reins in. Before him he sees a river, and the sun shining its last rays in that enchanting space between the black, looming clouds and the shadowed horizon. The water sparkles, and at the sight Niall laughs.

His laughter turns to shock as Anwyn bolts, without warning, toward the river. Niall loses the reins and is thrown back onto the horse's rump when Anwyn's first leaps nearly toss him to the ground. Niall hangs on as the gallop smoothes out and the Irishman barely manages to pull himself back into the saddle. The reins, though, which fly at the horse's side, are beyond his reach. So he lies forward along Anwyn's mane and, grasping the bridle straps, pulls back with all his strength. Finally, little more than a hundred yards from the river, Anwyn slows to a canter and at last to a slow trot. In this gait, Niall guides the horse onto the mud of the river's bank, where the thirsty horse lowers its head and drinks deeply. Niall jumps down, strips off his tunic and leggings, and runs shouting into the water. In seconds, he feels the thirst and the dust of the last many days fall from him like a shed burden.

The rain falls in sheets deep into the evening, and when it stops it is past midnight but Niall feels no need of rest. Readying Anwyn, he mounts and rides south along the river bank.

In the gray, cloudy morning, from the top of a hill, Niall looks across the river to an old, beaten pathway leading southwest. Crossing the river with great care, Anwyn having to swim the middle part, the Irishman scales the river bank and guides his mount onto the path. Obviously unused, perhaps for decades, it is overgrown with weeds and grass. Still, it clearly leads southwest, and it is just such a path that Merlin instructed him to look for. Niall follows it for several miles.

Finally, with the mid-afternoon sun lost in the thick clouds above, the traveler comes over the top of a steep grade and sees, less than a mile off, a ring of stones standing forsaken in a clearing. He urges Anwyn onward until they arrive at a narrow ditch crossing the path. Here Niall dismounts, readies his sword and shield, and goes forward. He jumps over the ditch, then over a fallen oak tree that lies across the pathway. The breeze has stilled.

The Irishman walks between two stones of the

outer ring. Like the pathway, they are long out of use, but they look only worn, not worn out. He passes a second ring of stones, then a third. In the center, he sees a stone taller than the rest and seemingly newer. It bears none of the signs of age, but instead looks almost new. It stands on a six-foot-high mound. Beside it lies an altar stone.

Niall stands in the center of the ring and looks about him. Nothing happens. Shrugging, he walks back to Anwyn and decides to wait until night, even though he does not like the thought of being near the stones in the moonlight. If Merlin was right, this is where he must be, so he might as well find out why. Keeping his weapons close at his side, he falls into a troubled sleep.

When he wakes the sky is dark, but no moon shines and no wind blows. Anwyn is grazing a few yards behind him, and the noise the horse makes is welcome in the night's silence. Niall gets up, slips his left arm through the bands on his shield, and fastens his sheath about his waist. He walks to Anwyn, drinks some water from the flagon, and eats some bread.

Suddenly, the Druidstones begin to glow: black, then dark blue, but not through the entire cycle. Now there is no brilliant blue, no green, no gold. From dark blue, the stones turn a deep red, all stones but one. In the center of the ring, the stone on the mound emits a black-red the color of blood. To this stone Niall knows he must go.

The silence of the night seems to sing in Niall's ears. The music is of suffering, or torment, of hatred . . . a music as dark as the blood color of the center stone. As Niall passes through the rings, the stones seem to shimmer and their light begins to block the sky. By the time Niall passes the innermost ring, he can no longer see the blackness above him. Fear in his throat, he turns his eyes towards the stone that marks the center of the innermost circle.

Impossibly, it glows black-red. It shines and yet it does not shine. It shimmers, but it is as still as death. And it beckons. To Niall, it is both the beacon of the harbor and the summons of the grave. Holding his breath, he walks up to the mound on which it stands.

Suddenly he sees, at the base of the mound, a hole, four feet in diameter, out of which issues a light of pale gold. This wasn't here earlier, he thinks; I'd never have stayed if it had been. But he senses, too, that it is too late to turn back, and he's not even sure that he wants to. The hole terrifies him, but the gold light looks so warm compared to the black-red of the center stone that he finds himself drawn toward it. At the edge of the hole he stops, looks one last time at the horror of the standing stone shimmering black-red in front of him, then crouches and, bracing his arms on the edge, lowers himself into the golden light.

The hole does not go straight down but forms a ramp running under the stone at a sixty-degree angle. Niall half crawls, half slides downwards, controlling his descent with his legs and balancing himself with his arms. In the light he can see the sides and the ceiling which, like the ramp itself, are made of stone. As the minutes go by, Niall gains confidence and speeds his descent.

But not for long. He notices the gold light growing,

and soon it is almost as bright as the light of early dawn. Then, without warning, the floor drops away and Niall's feet dangle over the edge of a large hole. He looks down but can see nothing, even though the light is as bright as a small fire. There is no way down, he thinks to himself, except to jump and hope a bottom comes up pretty quickly. If only he could see.

If Niall jumps, turn to section 19.

If he crawls back up the passageway, turn to section 16.

* **12** *

Niall moves first. He aims a quick slash at Redbeard's legs. Redbeard parries it, then jumps back. The two men circle, both watchful for a mistake. Suddenly Redbeard opens up the fight. With a yell, he charges.

Surprised but prepared, Niall ducks his opponent's high swing, then whirls and thrusts at Redbeard's back as he runs by. He draws blood, but not enough. Redbeard grunts, then turns and walks back to the fight. Over Redbeard's shoulder, Niall sees Blackbeard rising to his feet. *I must strike now*, he thinks. *Two may be too much.*

A leap into the middle, a parry of Redbeard's slash, a feint to the legs, and a cut to the head. More blood, and Redbeard staggers, but he is not out yet. Niall runs toward him, takes a small cut on the arm, and kicks his opponent in the groin. Redbeard doubles over and Niall runs him through.

A thrown knife misses Niall's ear by an inch. He looks up and sees Blackbeard staggering toward him, groggy from his earlier fall and weaponless without his knife. Niall raises his sword above his head, waits for the man to fall, and with both hands hurls the sword toward him. It is not a killing blow, striking the dark man's shoulder and, for a moment, pinning him to the ground.

The moment is all Niall needs. He runs to Redbeard, takes up the gleaming sword, and rushes back to the smaller man. The black-bearded man's scream is cut off abruptly as Niall's new sword slashes open his neck.

Exhausted from both the strain of the combat and his restless dreams, Niall lies motionless on the grass, wanting neither to get up nor to fall asleep. But when the first light of morning shows in the west, Niall knows that he must continue his journey across the plain of Salisbury to the standing Druidstones. His head throbbing and his eyes burning, he pushes himself to his knees and then to his feet. The dawn air is cool, a south wind brings the scent of the sea, and Niall feels himself beginning to revive.

Finding nothing of use on the dead men's bodies, he picks up Redbeard's sword and shield. Then, sheathing the sword and slinging the shield onto his back, he casts his own sword out of sight into the long grass. With his wooden shield, he covers the battered and bloodied face of the man with the black beard. At the sight of that face, and with the smell of death and blood now rising with the sun, Niall turns away, falls to his knees and vomits in the grass. Without looking again at the bodies, he saddles Anwyn, lays Merlin's sacks across the horse's back, then mounts and rides southwest across the green plain.

With the sword, Niall does 1 D6+3 points of damage. The shield decreases an enemy's To Hit number by 1. Note these numbers on your character record sheet.

Turn to section 11.

* **13** *

Yes, thinks Niall, a smile crossing his face. I can't see it, I can only see this damned light. The light won't let me see; light only helps if there is something to see. So all I have to do is get rid of the light. Since I don't know the source, the only way I can stop the light is to close my eyes. Once I'm blind, I should be okay.

Standing in front of the door's outline, Niall closes his eyes. He reaches out with his sword and feels the door is still there, so he sheathes the sword and stretches out his right arm. It meets no obstacle. With a soft laugh and his eyes shut tight, Niall walks through the open space.

Turn to section 14.

* **14** *

Niall finds himself in a tunnel constructed entirely of smooth, polished stone. A soft golden glow the brightness of early dawn illuminates the stone, but nothing ornaments the walls or floor. Niall waits for his eyes to focus in the partial darkness, then starts down the tunnel. A few yards ahead the light grows dimmer.

Into the dimness Niall now steps, his progress cautious and his mind filled with doubt. He does not know where he is going, nor whether or not he could leave this place now if he wanted to. And the desire to leave strengthens with each step as the gold light pales almost to darkness. Then, beneath his feet, the stone becomes rough, and he is forced to concentrate on the walking itself. The tunnel turns sharply to the right and, from around the corner, Niall sees a light glowing, a light the color of blood. He stops.

Well, Irishman, he thinks to himself, what do you do now? You're tired—not so tired that you can't walk, but getting there—and you've brought no food and no drink, and you don't even know where you are. If you somehow rose straight to the surface, you don't know if you'd come out in the center of the Druidstones or somewhere near Anwyn—and, by the gods to whom my people pray, no one better have touched that animal—or maybe you'd arrive in the bloody river. Now a red light the same color as the center stone waits for you around the corner, and you're more afraid than you've ever been in your life. What the hell are you doing here?

Section 15

His mission—and he scarcely remembers what that mission was—has ceased to hold any importance to him, as all missions do when they take on unforeseen danger and unrelieved terror. The red light draws him just as the center stone did, but all his training has been for survival not knowledge, and that training now tells him to turn back. The red light compels him to go on, but the gold light, even though it blinds, begins to pull him back. If he goes on, he may meet the specter of Uther Pendragon, or he may meet death. If he returns, he may get another chance, or he may have failed totally. Niall slumps to the floor and hides his head in his hands.

If Niall decides to go into the red light, turn to section 20.

If he decides to make his way back to Anwyn, turn to section 15.

* 15 *

Niall walks, climbing a long, steepening grade, refusing to look back over his shoulder at the red light, now pulsing, that fills him with terror. Through the long tunnel it tracks him, as the smooth stone walls dance in the red glow. Unwillingly, but unable to stop himself, he quickens his step, but the pulsing light deepens to black-red and does not falter.

At last, torn between terror and hopelessness, the Irishman turns. Toward him, barely distinct in the heart of the red light, rides a horseman astride a blood-red mount, a black sword in his left hand raised high above his head and a black shield obscuring the right side of his body. No eyes show in his face.

Niall draws his sword and holds it in front of him. It trembles. The horseman reins in his horse, then waits unmoving. The red light pulses, harsh, almost blinding. The silence is complete.

And then Niall breaks, and he feels himself begin to sob, and he hears his quavering voice yelling, pleading, "BE GONE, DAMN YOU! GO BACK!" Then he falls to his knees, buries his face in his arms and whispers, "In the name of Bran, leave me alone." As his tears flow and his eyes close, he waits for the end.

But it does not come. Instead, Niall's fear begins to subside, and the air begins to grow warmer. At last, gaining control himself, he slowly raises his head and opens his eyes. The horseman has turned and is riding away. Soon he is gone, and with him the red glow. The tunnel is now a deep blue, the color of night.

Niall rises and resumes his walk. The grade seems gentler now, and he feels strangely refreshed. Without difficulty, he finds the end of the tunnel and makes his way out. The route has changed: the blinding gold light is gone, and so is the hole he jumped through. Now there is only a long, steady grade that climbs for several hundred yards to finally emerge at the base of the central Druidstone.

The night is not yet old when Niall steps into the open air and away from the Druidstone. In the moonlight, he sees Anwyn grazing. The Druidstones stand dark and old in front of him; they are colorless and do not beckon. When Niall looks back at the center stone, he sees that the hole in the mound is no longer there.

Turn to section 16.

* **16** *

In his sleep, Niall hears the sound of hooves galloping toward him, faint at first, then growing louder as they approach. Into his dreams comes the specter of Uther Pendragon bearing the sword, shield, and helm of Arthur the king. The Pendragon's mouth is open as if to speak, but the image fades before it can utter a word.

Niall wakes, and the night is old. He hears nothing but the breeze whistling softly through the Druidstones. Still tired, he lays his head back down on the sack he uses for a pillow and begins to fall again into sleep.

Suddenly he hears, from deep beneath the earth, the sound of hooves. They begin as a walk, then a trot, and then a canter. Niall sits up. The sound has stopped. Putting his ear to the ground, he hears them again, now louder and faster. Shivering, he takes his sword and shield, readies them, and stands up. There is no sound.

Crouching down, he bends his ear to the earth once more. The hooves are loud now, and the horse is galloping hard. Louder they grow, then louder still, and soon they are like a drum pounding in his head. Again he raises his head, and again the sound stops. Then he lowers it, and the earth seems to shake with sound. Lifting his head, he looks to the Druidstone in

the center of the circle. It is pulsing with a blood-red glow. The pulse deepens as he watches until the red seems to burst apart with each beat. Now the red is brilliant, and all the Druidstones shine with reflection. Niall stands and watches.

Then suddenly, from out of a chasm that opens at the base of the center stone, Uther Pendragon comes forth into the world. In his right hand he carries aloft Caliburn the sword, and in his left the shield Pridwen, and on his head there shines a helm of gold graven with the semblance of a dragon. This is Arthur's father, thinks Niall, but he carries Arthur's things. The Irishman feels awe, and he is astonished, but he feels no terror. Before his eyes the color of the specter turns from red to gold, and the voice of Uther Pendragon rises quavering in the night. "Welcome, Death," it says, and the rider begins to charge.

If Niall chooses to fight, turn to section 28.

If he tries to evade the charging horseman, turn to section 25.

* **17** *

"Damn it," says Niall aloud, frustrated and disoriented in the unrelenting golden light. "I can't figure out how to get it open, may it rot in hell."

He gets up, explores the door's outline once more, then says, "Well, if I can't think my way through the door, maybe I can knock the damned thing down." From a distance of only a few inches, he slams the unseen door with his shoulder, but it does not move.

Backing up a few feet, he tries it again. This time he thinks it gives, but only a fraction of an inch. Finally, he backs up three yards and begins his charge.

Make a Strength roll. If an "S" is marked in the Special Events box of Niall's character record, increase his Strength by 1.

If the roll succeeds, turn to section 18.

If the roll fails, continue making Strength rolls until Niall succeeds. For each failed roll, Niall takes 2 points of damage. On the first successful roll, turn to section 18.

* **18** *

The door gives way, opening from bottom to top and shattering into splinters on the ceiling of the adjoining room. The splinters fall like daggers toward the startled Irishman.

Make a Dexterity roll. If Niall fails, he takes 1 D6+2 points of damage. If he succeeds, he rolls out of the way and suffers no damage. In either case, turn to section 14.

* **19** *

Niall lands almost as soon as he jumps, but on what he cannot tell. Beneath him and around him he sees only a golden light: no walls, no ceiling, no floor. Still he can walk, and he does so, hands stretched out before him to avoid walking into a wall. The precaution proves necessary as his outstretched fingers encounter a solid object. Turning to his left he touches another wall. Opposite this wall is yet another, which means he has discovered one end of this tunnel, if that's what it is. Keeping his shield arm against the lefthand wall, he walks away from the end wall using his sword as a cane on the floor in front of him. Soon the sword touches a wall and, running his hands along it, Niall feels the outline of a door. He pushes it, but it does not move.

He can feel no latches on the outside, nor any hinges. "If only I could see it," he says aloud, "maybe I could find a way to open it. Or at least figure out how to knock it down." He sits on the floor, which feels like warm marble, and thinks.

Make an Intelligence roll. If an "S" is marked in the Special Events box of Niall's character record, increase his Intelligence by 2.

If the roll succeeds, turn to section 13.

If the roll fails, turn to section 17.

* **20** *

Niall rounds the corner and squints his eyes against the throb of a blood-red light. The deep red covers the passageway in front of him, obscuring all as the golden light had done before. But this is not gold; this is red the color of blood, and it pulses toward him in a hypnotic rhythm. Like the red of the center Druidstone outside, this light beckons him forward.

Tired and frightened but desperate to understand, Niall steps into the redness.

At once a pounding, like a drum only inches from his ear, enters his head and turns away his sight. For several moments he sees nothing but the color of red. But his mind clears, even if his vision does not, and he takes another careful step forward. Now the light is brighter, but the noise is even greater than before. His head feels about to burst when he manages one more action, a final step into the center of the blood-red mass.

Now to his ears there comes a tremendous roar of sound, a cacaphony of unpatterned noise that assaults his mind even as it blocks out his senses. For here the pulse is faster than his brain can think, brighter than his eyes can see, louder than his ears can hear. And in the red mass are images he can barely comprehend: the bodies of soldiers rent to tiny pieces, the blood of sacrificial victims and slaughtered innocents, the armed might of Rome and the hate-filled fury of the naked, frenzied Saxons. But through all these images comes a larger image, an image much older, the image of the towering Druidstones in the setting sun. Above the stones rides always the image of Uther Pendragon bearing Caliburn, Arthur's sword, and Pridwen, Arthur's shield. On his head is the golden helm emblazoned with a dragon.

"Come," a voice calls through the red. "Come," it repeats, and Niall steps toward it.

With that step, the pounding stops and the color dims. Once again there is only a dull, blood-red glow in the passageway, and once again the passageway itself is visible. But now the glow shows a doorway,

Section 20

and through it Niall can make out the back of a huge figure seated motionless in the center of the room. Near the figure, on a stone slab, lies what looks like a body. Niall steps into the room.

The seated figure is covered with a blue robe. What it is, Niall cannot tell, but under the robe it seems to be holding out its arms in front of itself. The body on the stone slab lies under a purple robe stained black at one end with dried blood.

Suddenly, as Niall watches, the purple robe begins to glow very faintly, and the blood-stains change from black to dark red. Then it stops. A few minutes later, it does the same thing. Again it stops, and again starts. On and off, a long, regular pulse. The blue robe does nothing.

Make an Intelligence roll.

If it succeeds, turn to section 22.

If the roll fails, continue reading this section, choose one:

If Niall lifts the blue robe off the seated figure, turn to section 24.

If he lifts the purple robe off the body, turn to section 27.

* **21** *

Niall examines the rest of the body, but he finds nothing similarly strange. He hesitates, then starts toward the blue robe. He shudders as he draws closer.

Turn to section 24.

* **22** *

Niall recalls what has happened so far at the Druidstones. He followed the light that pulsed from the center stone, the golden light in the tunnel, and the throbbing red light in the passageway outside this chamber. Following the light has not killed him—not yet, anyway—but he has no way of knowing if it has helped. Now there is only a dull, periodic glow to lead him, and Niall is unsure of this one as well.

If Niall lifts the blue robe off the seated figure, turn to section 24.

If he lifts the purple robe off the body, turn to section 27.

* **23** *

"The same size," Niall says aloud. "The same size as the polished stone. I wonder . . ."

If Niall places the polished stone atop the burn marks on the body's chest, turn to section 33.

If he decides not to do so, turn to section 21.

* **24** *

Niall stands in front of the seated figure, just past the outstretched arms. Holding his breath, Niall reaches forward, grasps the blue robe in both hands and pulls hard. The robe falls away.

A huge figure, half-man and half-bear, sits on the floor unmoving, seemingly a statue. Its mouth is clenched and its upper lip raised to reveal bear's teeth. Its arms are covered with hair, and the hands are men's hands, but the fingers have claws. The torso is enormous; full chest muscles look chiseled under the black hair. Hair covers the neck and most of the head. The legs are those of a man, but they appear to be enormously strong.

Gripped in the man-bear's hands is the skull of a human. From it, gray skin droops loosely and long gray-brown hair hangs in strings. Moving slowly in fear and awe, Niall walks to his left, placing himself between the man-bear and the body on the stone slab. When he looks at the skull, he sees the mouth is open wide, paper-thin lips drawn back above old, brown teeth, the skull's eyes are little more than sockets. Sickened, Niall turns away.

Mastering himself once more, Niall steps toward the skull. He can take it from the man-bear's hands, he knows, but he knows as well that doing so might awaken the creature. He sees little hope in fighting the monster, which could kill him with one well-placed swipe of its claws. Still, his only other choice is to leave the tomb and return to Anwyn. This is likely the safest and perhaps the wisest course of action, but the idea grates on him as much as the skull's infernal howling. He takes a deep breath.

If Niall tries to take the skull from the man-bear, turn to section 31.

If he decides to leave the tomb, turn to section 16.

* 25 *

Diving to his right, Niall avoids the specter's first slash. The Irishman rolls, then springs to his feet and runs toward the hills. But the horseman has wheeled and, whirling Caliburn aloft, is now rapidly gaining on him. Again Niall leaps aside, this time getting up and racing toward the Druidstones. Still the specter pursues.

In and out among the Druidstones the chase goes on. Two stones fall shattering to the ground on impact with the charging horse, one barely missing the fleeing Irishman. But finally Niall is caught in the open, and the specter's horse knocks him to the

Section 25

ground with his hooves. Dazed, Niall staggers to his feet to face his opponent.

Use the combat rules to determine who wins the fight. To reflect the fact that the chase has tired Niall out, make a Constitution roll at the beginning of each round. If it succeeds, Niall fights normally. If it fails, decrease Uther's To Hit number by 3 and increase his To Be Hit number by 1. Remember to make this roll each round.

The horse will not attack unless Uther is killed. Uther will not dismount (which is why he is so difficult to hit). Niall can attack the horse instead of Uther. If the horse dies, decrease Uther's To Be Hit number by 3 and his To Hit number by 1 (it's easier to fight dismounted, but it's also easier to get hit).

THE GHOST OF UTHER PENDRAGON
To hit Niall: 15   To be hit: 5   Hit points: 32
Damage with sword: 2 D6−1

THE HORSE
To hit Niall: 13   To be hit: 12   Hit points: 58
Damage with hooves: 1 D6+3

If Niall wins, turn to section 26.

If Niall loses, turn to section 91.

* **26** *

The horse rears, high above the frightened Irishman. Niall jumps back, his reflexes making up for his astonishment. He examines his weapon but, majestic as it is, it cannot compare with Arthur's legendary sword, Caliburn. One thrust from Caliburn, Niall knows, and it will all be over.

Down swings Caliburn and Niall leaps for his life. He picks himself up off the ground but stumbles backward into a boulder. Leaping atop it, he braces himself and awaits Uther's charge. Running from the specter, he knows, is useless.

The charge comes quickly, and with it comes the battle cry of a soul in torment. So ghastly is it, so haunting, that Niall is frozen, his mind cleared of thought and his body shuddering. Down on the paralyzed Irishman sweeps the ghost of Uther Pendragon. At the last moment, Niall rips himself free from his terror and jumps. Pridwen misses him by scant inches.

He turns to face the horseman, a plan forming in his mind. As Uther sweeps by him, Niall waits for the exact second, then ducks under the legendary sword. He holds his own sword at waist height, and thrusts it out and upward to pierce the horse's chest.

Now for the hard part, Niall thinks. The horse can't last long, but he still has at least one charge in him. Niall must keep out of Uther's path. In an instant he spots a rough patch of rocky ground and runs to it as quickly as he can. There he turns and waits.

The horse charges, but its aim is untrue and its balance weak. It staggers into a run, then sways from its course. Niall gauges its path, standing where he thinks it will run.

The horse gains speed, but Niall stands his ground. If his plan fails, he is dead, but it gives him his only hope. He must defeat the horse, then he can fight the ghost.

The horse gallops, blood spraying from the wound in its chest. Then it stumbles, recovers, and stumbles again. Finally it leaps straight toward the Irishman, but its leap falls short and the horse's legs come down between two large rocks. Niall grimaces as he hears the bones snap. The horse falls, and beneath it falls Uther Pendragon.

Niall darts to the horse, draws out his sword, and faces the ghost, but there is no need. Uther lies silent, his fight gone. He turns strangely peaceful eyes toward his victorious foe.

"My time is up, warrior," says the body of Uther Pendragon as it lies motionless on the wet grass. "But you have done as I have long hoped. You have killed me, and for that I give my thanks. Now, perhaps, the gods will let me rest." The eyes close, and the wrinkles on the leathered skin seem to grow shallower and less harsh. Even the voice, thinks Niall, is softer.

But then suddenly, from the direction of the center stone, comes a roar that shatters the night calm. Shattered too is the new peace that, for a moment, had settled on Uther's body. Now Niall sees, carved on that ancient face, wrinkles like carved crevices and skin like gnarled wood. The eyes open again, and fear falls from them like dead leaves in the first wintry blast. Suddenly afraid, Niall steps back.

"Wait," says the dead man's voice, now ancient with its quaver. "Answer before you go. Why are you here? Why have you come this far looking for me? Answer quickly, for the beast approaches."

"Merlin sent me," Niall replies. "The specter of Uther Pendragon, he told me, would know of the goblet that Arthur is looking for."

"Would Arthur have you find this goblet?" the weakening voice asks.

"Yes. He sent me for it."

"Then listen. And when I have told you, go quickly. Do not watch what happens next.

"If there is a goblet, it is in a castle in Ireland, on an island near the western sea. The castle, it is said, is owned by a fisherman. My God, warrior, there is much more to tell, but no time. Go now. Hurry!"

"Wait," says Niall. "What else can you tell me? What castle? There are many . . ."

"GO!" shouts the body. "YOU ARE ALREADY CURSED!"

And then the night opens to the roar of the beast, and Niall feels it on his spine. Looking toward the center stone, he sees something rising from it, something huge, inhuman, terrible. It rises to its full height in the red glow of the Druidstone, then steps toward the fallen king and roars once more. As if in reply, Uther Pendragon screams, and the roar and the scream beat on Niall's ears until he can neither hear nor think. "GO!" shouts Uther Pendragon one last time, and Niall turns away and runs with all his speed.

Section 27

After running for what seems hours to him, Niall sees in the morning mist the form of a horse. The horse bolts at the sight of the man. "Anwyn," cries the Irishman. "Anwyn. Halt!" But Anwyn runs on, neighing in terror, until Niall loses him in the half-light of dawn. The Irishman stops, puts a hand to his aching side, and collapses to the ground. In terror and exhaustion, he vomits until he can no longer breathe, then he rolls into the long grass and falls into a dream-cursed sleep.

Turn to section 41.

* 27 *

Niall grasps the purple robe where the dried blood forms a hardened crust. As he begins to lift, the blood peels off onto his hands. Niall jumps back; the blood under the crust is still wet, and still warm.

Suppressing a shudder, the Irishman takes hold of the robe again, this time closing his eyes, and yanks it off the body. For a moment he holds his eyes shut. Slowly, he opens them to the sight of the naked, withered near-skeleton of what was once a man. The gray skin lies loose over prominent bones, and scars in the legs and chest attest to a harsh lifetime of wounds. Grisly as the sight is, Niall has seen similar corpses, and only one feature now captures his attention.

The body has no head. It has a neck, but no head. The smell of blood—old blood, but not dead blood— begins to fill the room. Niall steps closer. He sees that the head has been severed, maybe torn, from the neck just below the jaw line. Only the skull is gone.

Then he sees a string, thin almost as gossamer, around the headless neck. The two ends, both frayed, lie on the dead warrior's chest. Touching the string with his left hand, Niall finds the fabric smooth and cool, unlike any fabric he has ever known. It draws him, this touch, and for several minutes he runs his fingers along the string.

At last he shifts his eyes from the string to the chest beneath it. Thick, dark hair grown still thicker after death covers shrivelled, gray skin. Niall's fingers slip from the string and move down into this hair. It feels like bristles on top, but underneath it is still soft.

Niall's exploring fingers touch an indentation in the skin. Probing it with his fingers, he discovers it to be circular. Then, parting the hair with his right hand, he sees that the indentation is in fact a burn, almost like a brand.

If an "S" is marked in the Special Events box of Niall's character record, make an Intelligence roll. If the roll succeeds, turn to section 23. If it fails, turn to section 21.

If no "S" is marked in the box, turn to section 21.

* **28** *

Straight for Niall the horseman comes, lowering his blade like a lance with each passing step until it points at the Irishman's neck. Niall readies himself to spring from the attack, hoping to swing his sword as he jumps and injure his ghostly opponent.

Use the combat rules to determine who wins the fight. For the first round only, to simulate the charge, make a Dexterity roll. If it fails, Niall takes double damage that round. If the roll succeeds, Niall jumps out of the way and takes no damage. In this case, make a second Dexterity roll. If this one succeeds, Niall gets a free attack this next round.

The horse will not attack unless Uther is killed. Uther will not dismount (which is why he is so difficult to hit). Niall can attack the horse instead of Uther. If the horse dies, decrease Uther's To Be Hit number by 3 and his To Hit number by 1 (it's easier to fight dismounted, but it's also easier to get hit).

THE GHOST OF UTHER PENDRAGON
To hit Niall: 14   To be hit: 4   Hit points: 32
Damage with sword: 2 D6 – 1

THE HORSE
To hit Niall: 13   To be hit: 12   Hit points: 58
Damage with hooves: 1 D6 + 3

If Niall wins, turn to section 26.

If he loses, turn to section 91.

* **29** *

There is nothing else. Nothing past the hopeless words that form on the Irishman's lips. Nothing past the wordless songs that sing in his ears and block out the noise of the world. Nothing past the knowledge, now, that time begins its slow retreat back through the years he has lived, back through the long and fearless days he once had dared to call his own.

Now all is one. Light is dark. Hot is cold. Sleep is wakefulness. War is peace. Sight is blindness, and hearing the task of the deaf. Earth and stars and ocean fly apart into a black and formless void.

Into Heaven? Into Hell? If Niall could think, these would be his thoughts. He knows now what in life he had come to disbelieve: after death there is something. But Heaven? Hell? Which, he does not know. On he walks, his body forgotten already, toward a newness he cannot begin to comprehend.

There is nothing else. Something beckons; he follows. There is nothing else.

THE END

Turn to section 30.

* **30** *

A Note to the Reader

For now, Niall's adventure is over. But *Storm of Dust* is not a traditional novel; it can be played many times, to different endings. There are several ways to do this.

The first way, and the most complete, is to start over from the beginning. This means going back to Section 2 and making your choices from there. Remember, even if you make the same choices as before, the ending may be different. Niall may win a fight instead of lose, or he may discover something based on a dice roll.

The second way saves time, especially if you have progressed quite far into the novel. Look at the Special Events box of Niall's character record. Match the letters that appear there with the letters shown below and start from the indicated section.

Storm of Dust has several possible endings. Each has its own appeal (except for getting killed outright). Every time you reach an end, you will be directed to this section and you can start over. That way, you will eventually read every section in the book, and you can decide for yourself which ending you find most satisfying.

IF SPECIAL EVENTS BOX SHOWS:	RESUME AT SECTION
None	2
S only	41
S and M	55
S, M, and W	57
S, M, and L	51
S, M, W, and L	69
S, M, W, and B	57
S, M, L, and B	55
S, M, W, L, and B	77
Any combination without S	2
S plus any combination without M	41

* **31** *

The Irishman grasps the skull in both hands. Then, watching both beast and skull, Niall extracts the skull from the man-bear's hands. It slides out smoothly, and Niall stands for a moment looking at it closely. The tomb is completely silent.

Niall carries it to the stone slab and examines the body. Yes, he thinks, it will fit; it belongs to this body. He bends to place it atop the neck. A deep, rumbling roar begins to echo through the tomb. Niall snaps his head to the left and looks straight at the man-bear, which is slowly coming to life. It struggles, he sees, but then it starts to rise.

If Niall drops the skull to prepare for combat with the man-bear, turn to section 38.

If Niall puts the skull in place, turn to section 39.

* **32** *

During combat with the man-bear in section 36, the body eventually joins the fight on Niall's side. At the start of each round, make a Wisdom (Luck) roll. If it succeeds, the body begins fighting two rounds later. For example, if the Wisdom roll succeeds at the start of the second round, the body joins the fight at the start of the fourth round.

The body enters the fight bearing a gleaming sword. Use the man-bear's To Hit and To Be Hit numbers for attacks by the body as well as by Niall. (Note that these numbers may already be modified.) The body does one more point of damage than Niall. Both Niall and the body may attack once each round.

Once the body joins the fight, roll 1 d6 before each attack by the man-bear. On a 1 or 2, it attacks the body. On a 3–6 it attacks Niall. The body cannot be killed (it is already dead), and therefore has no hit points. It helps Niall by attacking the man-bear and by absorbing some attacks.

Turn to section 36.

* ✳ **33** ✳ *

Taking the polished stone from his boot, Niall examines it in the room's red glow. Still the lines are indistinct, and still he cannot read them. Then slowly, hesitantly, he lays the stone on the body's chest, precisely over the round burn. The fit is exact.

Imperceptibly at first, then becoming more and more visible, the stone begins to glow. At first it is nearly black, then a deep violet, and finally a brilliant, shining purple. Almost unbelieving, Niall stands back.

The lines glow too, and they are red. Black-red to begin, then blood-red, then a bright, sharp red the color of sunset. For the first time, Niall can see what the lines depict. Before his eyes they become the image of a bearlike man holding a skull. The skull wears a garland of flowers like a crown. The image pulses, grows brighter, pulses faster and then goes out. The purple glow fades from the stone.

Section 34

And then, from what seems the depths of the earth, a deathlike howl pierces the stillness of the tomb. Everywhere it echoes, and the echoes increase as the howl grows louder. Purely in reflex, Niall's hands slam against his ears, but they do little to protect him. On and on it goes, and Niall's head throbs in response.

Suddenly the Irishman lifts his head. Either the howl is softer, or else he has begun to grow used to it, but it sounds now as if it has a source. Taking his hands from his ears, Niall scans the room. Seconds pass, and the howl lessens. Seconds more, and it is lower still. Finally, Niall knows its source.

The howl is coming from under the blue robe. As soon as Niall takes one step toward the seated figure, the howl stops. The tomb is now quiet as death.

If Niall decides to lift the blue robe, turn to section 24.

If he decides to leave the tomb, turn to section 16.

* **34** *

The bolts have stunned the man-bear and damaged it as well. During the combat, described in section 32 and section 36, Niall gets two or three free rounds before the man-bear fights back. Roll 1 D6. If you roll 1–3, he gets two swings; on a 4–6, he gets three. After the free rounds, combat continues normally.

Turn to section 32.

* **35** *

As the huge beast lumbers toward him, Niall draws his sword and turns to face it. He knows it is strong, and he must stay out of its reach. Backing away from it, he extends the sword as far as he can in front of him, hoping the beast will grab for it. If it does, he can thrust hard into its chest.

Seeing the sword, the man-bear slows. Then it snarls, and the snarl chills Niall's blood. But he does not waver. He backs up one step, then another, then still another, as he holds the bear at bay.

He steps backward but suddenly he runs out of room. The stone slab presses into his back. He slides slowly along it to his right, then stops and waits. *Hold*, he tells himself. *Wait for just the right . . .*

With wicked, yellow claws extended, the bear's arm swings toward him, its speed wholly unexpected. The Irishman ducks, but the force of the blow throws him across the room. Niall shakes his head, gets up, and approaches the beast, which stands and waits for Niall to come within range.

This time, Niall is on the offense. *A better position*, he tells himself. Niall moves slowly so the beast is not startled into a sudden attack, and waits for the precise moment.

When the Irishman strikes, he aims a lightning thrust to the man-bear's neck. It slashes the animal, but no blood spills. The man-bear retaliates with a blow to Niall's ribs. Only the close quarters prevent the warrior's lung from being punctured.

Niall presses on, swinging his sword and landing

Section 35

blow after bloodless blow. Finally, after what seems like hours of fighting, the beast's time is over.

As the man-bear collapses motionless on the floor, Niall sees the head it once held lying ten yards away. Unsteady on his feet, weak from the fight, the Irishman walks to the head and picks it up. From it, gray skin droops loosely and long gray-brown hair hangs in strings. The mouth is open wide as if in the middle of a scream, paper-thin lips are drawn back above old, brown teeth. The skull's eyes are little more than sockets. Sickened, Niall turns his head away.

Mastering himself once more, he carries the skull to the stone slab and lays it atop the body's neck. As the skull touches the body, the skin of the neck begins to adhere to it, holding it in place. His mouth open in astonishment, Niall watches as head and body merge. He blanches with the strange, sickening smell of bones attaching and blood vessels reforming. Suddenly, the body begins to stir.

The mouth closes. The skin firms. The eyes open. And then a voice sounds, cold and deathly.

"I could have helped," it says, perhaps to no one. "But it is over." Then the head lies back, and the body is motionless once more.

Turn to section 93.

* **36** *

*Use the combat rules to determine who wins the fight.
The man-bear fights to the death.*

THE MAN-BEAR (AND BODY)
*To hit Niall: 12   To be hit: 9   Hit points: 65
Damage with claws: 1 D6+2*

If Niall wins, turn to section 40.

If he loses, turn to section 29.

* **37** *

Niall feels a hand grip his shoulder. Dropping to the
floor, he rolls to his right, then jumps up and turns
toward the body. In the tomb's red glow, the dead
warrior is struggling to sit up, its gray-brown hair
falling over its face and its skin flapping. Groggily, it
reaches toward the Irishman, who stands terrified at
the sight of the bony hand scant inches from his face.

But then he notices the body's other hand points
toward the man-bear. The beast staggers toward the
stone slab. Shaking, the body's hand straightens its
fingers and seems to wait for the man-bear to come
closer. Half in fear, half in shock, Niall watches the
scene as if from afar.

The man-bear steps closer, then closer still. The
body does nothing. Another step, then another. Still
the hand remains motionless. Then, with the man-
bear almost upon it, the body acts. Out from its

fingers and into the monster's eyes crimson bolts fly. The man-bear's roar turns to a scream as it tears at eyes now red the color of fire. As suddenly as they began the bolts now stop, and the body collapses onto the stone slab. The man-bear lumbers about in pain, its hands still covering its eyes.

If Niall attacks immediately, turn to section 34.

If he waits to see what happens, turn to section 32.

If he runs out of the tomb, turn to section 16.

* **38** *

Use the combat rules to determine who wins the fight. The man-bear will fight to the death.

THE MAN-BEAR
To hit Niall: 12   To be hit: 9   Hit points: 65
Damage with claws: 1 D6+2

If Niall wins, turn to section 35.

If he loses, turn to section 92.

* **39** *

As the skull touches the body, the skin of the neck begins to adhere to it, holding it in place. His mouth open in astonishment, Niall watches as head and body merge. He blanches with the strange, sickening smell of bones attaching and blood vessels reforming. Suddenly, the body begins to stir.

But the roar of the man-bear comes again to Niall's ears, and the Irishman turns around. The beast is now standing and turning slowly toward him. Unsteady on its feet but gaining strength with each second, it begins its advance. Niall draws his sword with his right hand and readies his shield on his left arm. The man-bear lumbers forward.

If Niall has placed the polished stone, turn to section 37.

If he has not, turn to section 32.

* **40** *

As the huge beast lumbers toward him, Niall draws his sword and turns to face it. He knows it is strong, and he must stay out of its reach. Backing away from it, he extends the sword as far as he can in front of him, hoping the beast will grab for it. If it does, he can thrust hard into its chest.

Seeing the sword, the man-bear slows. Then it snarls, and the snarl chills Niall's blood. But he does not waver. He backs up one step, then another, then still another, as he holds the bear at bay.

But suddenly he runs out of room. The stone slab presses into his back. He slides slowly along it to his right, then stops and waits. *Hold*, he tells himself. *Wait for just the right . . .*

With wicked, yellow claws extended, the bear's arm swings toward him, its speed wholly unexpected. The Irishman ducks, but the force of the blow throws him across the room. Niall rolls to his right, expecting the bear to press the attack, but it merely stands by the slab and waits.

Slowly the body rises from the stone slab to stand in front of the man-bear. It holds a gleaming, almost glowing sword in its hand. Seeing that glow, the bear growls in fear and anger. Niall watches, mesmerized, as the body swings the sword into the bear's side. With a howl, the bear strikes at the body and hits. The body backs up into the slab.

Niall rises and approaches from the beast's flank. With the man-bear's attention now diverted, Niall lifts his sword with both hands and swings down hard. Into the man-bear's neck it goes, but the head does not fall.

A back-hand blow knocks Niall off his feet, and he gasps for breath as he struggles to rise. He sees the body attack once more, and the gleaming sword bites deep into the beast's chest. Niall gets up to stagger back into the fight, shouting as he swings once more. This time it ends. The beast falls.

Turn to section 93.

* **41** *

The trip to his homeland in search of the grail is long, and Niall likes little of it. He feels trapped in a ship completely foreign to him despite its owner's claims that it is as Irish as he was. Totally unlike the skin-covered curraghs he had ridden in as a child, this ship seems unsteady in the water, swaying with the wind and wavering off course at the least sign of distress. Niall, who is rarely sick in boats, spends most of the journey lying on a blanket, trying to stop his stomach from heaving. At last he can stand it no longer, and he decides to ask the owner some questions.

The owner, like all men who spend their lives at sea, is gnarled, with leather skin and deep creases in his forehead and around his eyes. His lips are chapped as if they had been so since birth, and his voice is as rough as his skin. He is a man of the sea; he belongs there and he wants everyone to know it. For all his rough exterior, he is a man who commands respect, and Niall approaches him with some caution. When Niall finally manages to get the ship owner to stay in one place long enough to talk to him, the owner is intently examining a water-soaked rope for flaws while he shouts orders to his crew.

"A minute," says Niall. "I'd like to talk to you."

"Well," the owner replies. "Only for a minute. I'm busy, as you can see."

"There are a few things I'd like to know about your ship."

"Ah," exclaims the owner. "Excellent. Too few passengers care to know anything about the ship that carries them. What would you like to know?"

Niall hesitates a moment, trying to frame the question. "First," he begins, "why does it feel unsteady?"

The owner creases his brow as if insulted. "Unsteady?" he snarles. "I don't find it unsteady at all."

"Well, then," says Niall, "why does it seem to sway back and forth almost as if it has no keel?"

The captain laughs. "That's simple. It feels that way because it *has* no keel. None at all."

Niall starts. "But how . . . ?"

"A ship needs no keel," the owner interrupts. "Not if it is driven properly. And without a keel, the ship is more maneuverable, especially in battle."

"Battle?" Niall asks. "This ship has seen battle?"

"You seem surprised. Why?" Again, the owner seems insulted.

"It hardly seems steady enough," blurts out Niall.

The owner stares at Niall for a time, then takes one step toward him. Niall prepares to back away, but the owner stops, seems to master himself, and mutters, "Maybe you'll live long enough to learn something about it." The way he says "maybe" makes Niall wary.

The Irishman feels a spray of sea water across his back, then says to the owner, "I'm sorry if I insulted you. It wasn't meant."

"It never is," replies the owner. "Now I must get back to work." Niall watches him walk away. Before he takes a dozen steps, he turns, looks at the Irishman and shakes his head. Finally, Niall walks back to his pallet on the deck.

The rest of the trip passes uneventfully, but Niall continues to be wary. The owner passes him rarely, but when he does he looks at him with suspicion. Nothing happens, but Niall does not even doze for the rest of the journey.

Now, as he walks along the coast, with the sea crashing against the rocks to the east and the spray wetting his hair as it did on the unsteady ship, Niall recalls the journey and wonders still at the wisdom of having a ship without a keel. But he feels, too, as the miles crawl by under his feet, that maybe his own journey, even though it is on land and not at sea, is also without a keel. He is able to steer himself and he is able to stay afloat, but just barely. His journey seems to be taking place without him, as it has ever since he started. Not at any point in his wanderings, he thinks, has he felt in control of what he was doing.

Merlin sent him on this search; he did not send himself. He is not even sure, at this point, if he would have started the journey without the wizard's prodding. He remembers the night when Merlin visited his tent and he remembers the fight with Lancelot, but he does not remember ever making the decision to begin. Merlin came and packed his bags and sent him away. Niall himself seemed to have nothing to do with it.

And now, at long last, he is in charge of his own fate, and is not at all sure he likes the feeling. He is not proud of his accomplishments so far, but at least he has made some progress. Now, with the toughest part of the journey facing him, and with virtually no idea where he is to go, he suddenly appreciates the wizard's early guidance even though at the same time he resents it. There is something comforting about being told what to do, especially when you are uncertain of the best path of advance. Merlin took away his responsibility, but he also took away the problem of choice. Now he is faced with both, and the weight of responsibility is heavy.

The sound of galloping hooves jars him from his thoughts. Niall quickly looks behind, then runs off the road into the long grass of a crudely dug ditch. His hand sinks into mud and his boot fills with cold, dirty water. Miserable and cold, he waits for whatever it is that approaches.

What approaches, in fact, is two horses, not just

one. On the first rides a man of medium height but muscular build, black hair streaming behind him and a sword sheathed at his left side. Beside him rides an enormous figure, as large as any man Niall has ever seen. The two gallop toward Niall's hiding spot. Suddenly, just as they are upon it, they rein in and start to look around them. Niall does not stir.

"I'm not sure, my friend," the smaller man says. "We were told of his passing along this road, but nobody gave us specific directions. I'm a poor tracker, especially when I'm in a hurry."

"And I'm not one at all, Irishman," the big man's gravel voice replies, "hurry or no. I still don't understand what the hell we're doing here. You say 'Follow me,' and you expect me to follow. And usually, ass that I am, I do, but sometimes I like to know why. Does this one man matter so much?"

"It depends," replies the other, "on whom you're asking. Starkad, old friend, I've never led you on a wild goose chase before. Why is it so hard to believe me now?" The smaller man laughs, but the larger just snorts.

"You know best, I suppose," he says, "when you know at all. But we've been chasing this person for two days now, and I'm tired. And more than a little hungry, too. Don't you ever stop?"

"No. Not till I'm done, and neither do you. Now, where to next? I think he's probably headed along the coast. At least, that's how he started. Should we keep going this way?"

The big man laughs, then slips off his horse and lands on the ground. "At last you admit it, Irishman," he says. "You don't know. Good. That means I can have a rest."

The smaller man looks down from his horse, and already his companion is stripping off his pack and laying a huge axe on the ground. "Perhaps you're right," he says as he dismounts. "There's little point in continuing on this way. Still, I wish Veleda had told us more, and I wish even harder that she had come with us. Maybe she'd know where to find him."

The giant sits up at the sound of that name. "I'm not so sure." He pauses. "At times I think she's the most brilliant woman in the world, but then she turns around and makes us do something like this. I know you're obsessed with her, but sometimes I think she takes away your ability to think. You used to have that, you know." He lays his head back on the ground.

"Hardly fair, Starkad," says his partner, and his voice sounds a little perturbed. "She's never led us astray, and I think you know that. If not for her, I don't think we'd have stayed together this long. Hell, we might have killed each other first."

"I doubt it," the giant replies. "Besides, that's not what I mean. Do you think I'm jealous of her because you have a woman every night and I don't? I'm not like some ridiculous wife, Irishman, who can't stand to see her husband's time taken up with anyone else, man or woman. That's got nothing to do with it. But since you met her we seem worse off than we ever have. We spent a year in Gaul and what do we have to show for it? I nearly get my balls shot off by some German's arrows, and you get your back sliced up by an idiot who can't tell an Irishman from a Saxon. We lose our money three times, our horses twice, and four times we end up fighting a war against some enemy we don't know and might not even care about.

And not even that gets us any money. Hell, we had more money when we left than we do now, and fewer scars."

"And what's Veleda got to do with that?" the Irishman asks. His voice bears a tinge of acid.

"Calm down," says the giant. "No point getting upset about it. Maybe nothing. Probably nothing. But we never had these scraps before, and we certainly never did anything like this before. This is just fucking stupid, and you know it."

The smaller man laughs as he sinks cross-legged to the ground, obviously amused with his friend's words. "Never done anything like *this* before?" he cries. "You fight a bunch of Arthur's bloody Companions, and you watch me bring back an impossible skull, and you help me fight off an entire village before you decide to rescue me from a crypt where I'm fighting something I don't even understand, and then you help me beat a dragon, a dragon with no end of strength and created by magic. And then you say we haven't done anything like this before?" He throws back his head and laughs hard and clear. The giant does not move.

"Besides, old friend," the Irishman continues, "we're not here to fight dragons or to show up a Companion or to capture a skull. We're here to find a man. Just one man, and an Irishman at that. That's all. We have to ask him some questions and we have to relay a message to him. I don't understand why it's got you all upset. We've been to worse places and we've done worse things. Why now?"

For a time the giant does not reply. Then, slowly, he lifts himself onto his elbows and stares at the smaller man. "Mael," he says, "I don't think you'll ever understand why I feel the way I do. We've fought together, we've lived together, and we even used to have women together, but you've never really got through to the Dane in me, I guess." He pauses. "I never used to know what they were talking about when they said men from different places will always be different. I guess I'm beginning to. It bothers me because I don't think it should be that way."

The Irishman looks down at the ground. He thinks for a while, then scratches his head and looks up. "Starkad," he says, "what are you talking about? I've never seen you like this."

In response, the giant leaps to his feet. "I don't know," he says. "Feeling sorry for myself, I guess. Let's get out of here."

"Good idea," says the Irishman as he untangles his legs to stand. "But I wish we knew where to find this person we're looking for, this Niall mac Llyr. I really don't know why Veleda wants him, but she does. And he's one of the reasons we're here." He climbs into his saddle easily, then waits for the giant to mount and says, "But you're right. We'll try someplace else."

Niall listens to this entire exchange, knowing now that he is the man they are looking for. He has heard of Mael mac Ronan and Starkad the Dane, but he has never seen them before. He is puzzled about how they know him and what Veleda, Mael's woman, wants to tell him. What worries him most of all are the questions they want to ask him. How, he wonders, will this affect his mission? And what, if anything, does it have to do with the goblet? Maybe nothing, but he isn't sure.

As they prepare to leave, with Mael's horse taking

its first steps forward, Niall must decide whether to show himself or to let the pair leave. "I'm ready," says the Dane. "Let's go."

If Niall reveals his presence, turn to section 43.

If he remains hidden, turn to section 55.

If Niall reveals his presence, turn to section 43.

If he remains hidden, turn to section 55.

* **42** *

Niall unsheaths his sword and turns towards the horseman. The horse rears on its hind legs and neighs in an otherworldly voice. Niall shivers with sudden fear.

Suddenly Mael steps in front of Niall and walks toward the horseman. "No!" shouts Niall as he reaches for his companion. But the horseman brings down his whip, and at the crack Mael cries out and covers his face. "My eyes!" he screams. "My eyes. My eyes. My eyes . . ."

Niall has no time to tend to him. The horseman has raised his whip again, and now the horse advances. Niall steps back, his eyes fixed on the handle of the black whip. The horseman sits motionless, and Niall stands and waits.

Use the combat rules to determine the winner. The horseman attacks with his whip only. He does not use the horse to kick, trample, or charge. Mael does not enter the battle. Niall can damage the horseman only with his sword. He cannot damage the horse at all.

THE HORSEMAN
To hit Niall: 13   To be hit: 5   Hit points: 48
Damage with whip: 1 D6+4

The horseman gets one crack of the whip every two rounds beginning with the first round.

If, in any round, the horseman obtains a damage result of 10 (rolls a 6), make a Dexterity roll. If it succeeds, Niall ducks under the whip and takes normal damage. If it fails, Niall is struck in the eyes. In that case, Niall must make a Constitution roll each round thereafter. If the Constitution roll succeeds, Niall fights normally for that round. If the roll fails in any round, turn to section 56.

If Niall defeats the horseman, turn to section 52.

If Niall is defeated, turn to section 29.

* **43** *

"Wait," Niall shouts as he rises from the ditch. He shakes the cold mud from his hands, straightens his clothes, and musters all his calm to step without nervousness onto the road.

At the sound of his voice, the two mounted men wheel their horses around. Niall sees the giant grasp the handle of his axe, and he sees the Irishman grip the reins tightly. Finally the smaller man says, "Who are you? What do you want?"

"My question, I'm afraid," says Niall. These men, he realizes, will not be impressed unless he shows defiance. Even then, they may not be impressed, but he feels he must take the chance.

"What do you mean, *your* question? I asked it, not you." Mael's voice is stern, commanding. Niall knows he must not wilt under its force.

"Yes, but it wasn't your place. It was mine, and now I choose to ask it. I turn the question back to you. Who are you and what do you want?" Niall stares into his countryman's eyes.

Mael waits for a moment, and the Dane starts to fidget. Plainly, Niall thinks, this isn't going to work for long.

Finally the smaller man speaks again. "Oh, all right. What difference does it make?" He turns to his companion. "This isn't getting us anywhere, my friend. We'll tell him our names. If he doesn't do the same, we'll kill him. Then it won't matter anyway."

He looks at Niall. "I'm Mael mac Ronan, but I'd appreciate your not telling anyone else, at least no one in Ireland. Some people don't want me here. This," he points at his companion, "is Starkad the Dane, Thurid's son. He's very strong."

Niall begins to smile at this last comment, sure Mael means to joke, but neither Mael nor Starkad changes expression. Instead, he looks up the road, crouches down to knock a clump of mud off his boot, and stands up again. "That's one answer," he says. "Now what about the other? What do you want?"

"What we want, ass, is our business." Mael seems taken aback at Niall's failure to identify himself.

Niall pauses, but he feels himself tensing. The Dane is beginning to look very impatient. "It *was* your business," he says at last, "until you talked about *me*. Then it became mine." He watches for a response, but the horsemen show none. This can't go on much longer, he thinks again.

"We talked about no one," Mael finally replies.

"Not true, I'm afraid," Niall says.

The Dane looks at Mael, and Mael nods. "Yes," the Irishman says. "You're right. We did talk about someone. Are you Niall mac Llyr, then?"

Niall looks directly at his mounted countryman. "What do you know of him?"

"I asked you a question," Mael replies. "Are you Niall mac Llyr?"

Niall stands tensed, trying to draw out his advantage one more precious minute. Soon he will have to give it up, and he might suffer for it. He thinks his arrogant stance has been worthwhile, but there is no way he can be sure. One more minute, he thinks, will serve him well. All he hopes is that the men do not attack him.

"I said I am the man you spoke of. Isn't that enough?"

Finally the Dane breaks his silence. "Damn it!" he shouts. "I've had enough of these games. Are you Niall mac Llyr, or aren't you?" He leaps from his horse, his hand on his axe handle. "Tell us now and make it plain, or I'll drive your balls up into your throat." He takes one step towards the Irishman.

Niall does not move. He hadn't expected this, but he wasn't ready to concede the advantage yet. Still, the danger is suddenly real. The Dane is angry enough to kill him.

Starkad takes another step. Niall stays where he is. Another step. Still Niall refuses to move. Starkad raises his axe into the air. He takes one more step.

Niall waits, his blood pounding in his head. One more step, giant, just one. One more bloody step. The Dane's arm muscles ripple as they clench the handle of the axe. The two men stare at each other, neither blinking, neither giving way. Niall counts the beats of his heart. And then, finally, the Dane takes another step.

With that step, Niall makes his move. He shrugs,

turns, and walks up the road. From the giant comes a low growl.

His back turned, Niall suddenly feels in great danger. For a moment all is silent and tense. Then he hears the voice of the smaller man, and it is laughing. The laugh starts slowly, then grows by the second, and finally fills the silence of the scene. Softer than the laugh is the long, raspy growl of Starkad the Dane.

"He got you there, my friend," Mael says as his laugh finally subsides. "I haven't seen you look that foolish since you ripped apart your leg trying to get at that wench in the witch's house." He laughs again, then shouts to Niall, "Wait, Irishman. You win. This round, at least. Now come and have some food. My friend won't poison it. I promise you that." He laughs again, then dismounts and walks towards Niall, his arm extended in a gesture of welcome. Niall shrugs again, then clasps his countryman's arm and walks with him back to the horses.

The meal is small, but it is far from bad. Dried biscuits, cakes, pieces of fresh meat, fresh apples, and bread that isn't yet hard. And wine, which Mael refuses to drink but Starkad gulps. They eat with very little talk, then Starkad rises to feed the horses. Finally, with the sun low in the west, they light a small fire and lie on the ground about it. Niall has nearly dozed off by the time Mael asks his first question.

"What are your dealings with Arthur, Irishman?" he asks.

Niall is surprised at the directness of the question. "I don't think it's right that I tell anyone. I'm sworn to secrecy. At least, I think I am."

"I thought so. But Arthur is usually more forceful

than that. When I ran errands for him there was no question of secrecy. If I'd told anyone, he'd have killed me. It was that simple."

"My errand, too," replies Niall, "is secret. That's clear. But Arthur, in the end at least, wasn't the one who sent me away. Merlin did." Damn, he thinks to himself, why did I say that? This is probably the kind of thing they're trying to get out of me. More care. More care. But I'm tired.

"Merlin?" asks Mael. "That damned wizard? You let *him* tell you what to do? What the hell were you thinking, man?" The smaller man's eyes half close in anger.

Now the Dane laughs. Not long or loud, but a laugh nevertheless. "You're the foolish one this time, Mael. Don't think anything of it, Irishman. My friend's hated Merlin ever since the wizard insulted his whore. Very reasonable he is, until someone mentions the wizard." He laughs again.

"We'll have to have a talk, Starkad," says Mael, calm again, "but not right now. I want to find out more from our visitor here."

"I'm afraid," Niall replies, "that I don't have much to say. I've told you that the wizard sent me on this trip, at least that he got me started. I've also told you that my mission for Arthur is secret and that I'm not supposed to tell anyone about it. I don't think your questions will get you anywhere."

"Maybe not," Mael replies. "But let me try in any case. I'm not asking you to tell me where you're going and why—even though I'd very much like to learn that—but I still have to know a few things before I tell you what I was told to tell you. So answer as well as you can."

Niall looks at the man. He has no age, he thinks to

himself. He could be twenty-five or he could be forty. The Dane looks older but stronger, too. He hopes to fight neither; Mael may be smaller than the Dane, but he is still six feet tall and in peak fighting condition. Answering Mael's statement of intent, Niall nods.

"First of all, Niall, tell me directly: did Arthur send you on a mission?"

"Yes," Niall replies.

"Good. At least that is certain. Now, do you have any idea how much of the mission is his idea and how much is the wizard's?"

The question surprises Niall. "No, although Merlin was certainly jumpy while I talked with Arthur. But, no, I don't know. Why?"

"It might be important. That's all. But let's go on. Was Arthur frightened in any way at all? Did he act as if something was out of control?"

Niall thinks for a moment, because here he might reveal something. Finally he speaks. "No, Arthur didn't appear frightened. He seemed anxious but not fearful. But . . ." Niall hesitates. "Merlin seemed frightened."

"Merlin?!" This time it is the Dane who speaks. "The wizard was afraid? I've never seen him truly afraid. I'm sorry I missed it." A smile crosses his lips.

"Starkad, old friend," says the smaller man, "shut up. We're trying to get information, not show our visitor whom we like and whom we hate." The Dane glares at him for a moment, then lowers his head.

Mael continues. "Are you sure it was fear you saw and not—well, desire of some kind?"

"Desire?" asks Niall. "I don't understand."

"I can see why. Desire isn't the right word, perhaps. Are you sure Merlin wasn't simply anxious to get something. So anxious that he was willing to send even an outsider to get it?"

"Ah. That's what we're getting at. Why me and not one of the Companions? I don't see how that matters."

For a moment Mael is lost in thought. Then he says, "It doesn't. That's not what I meant. I've already figured out why you and not one of the Companions. You're Irish, and only the Irish can get around properly, and secretly, in Ireland. I've been used for the same reason. But Merlin—did he say why the mission was so necessary?"

"If I told you that, Mael, I'd be telling you the mission itself. If that's what you're trying to get out of me, you'll have to do better." Niall grins, and Mael returns it.

"Clumsy, yes. But that's not what I'm trying to do. It's Merlin I'm interested in, and Arthur. Not you, and not particularly your mission. Still, it's plain that you won't tell me much about it." He turns to the Dane. "What do we do now, Starkad?"

The giant grumbles. "Veleda wants us to give him a message, doesn't she? Why are you wasting all this time asking questions? Why not just give him the message?"

Mael shakes his head, then says, "You're right. I just want to be sure we've got the right person here. And I'm trying to figure out Veleda's plans as well. And Merlin's. And Arthur's, if he has any. It's important to understand him. He is very powerful."

"Yes," says Starkad. "But as long as we stay on the good side of his power, it won't affect us. The man has great sway over his Companions and even over the tribes who fight for him. He even has sway over us, my friend. But I don't think he has any power at all over Veleda. She is her own woman, and she doesn't need Arthur—or you—one bit. You've seen her, Mael, and yet you still have no idea how much power she has. Why didn't you ask *her* about Merlin? She could have told you."

"Perhaps," replies Mael. "But she wouldn't have. She holds secrets. From me, and from all the world. I don't like that, but there seems nothing I can do about it."

"Exactly. So why bother trying?"

Niall watches the two friends and feels suddenly lonely.

The Dane continues. "Now, old friend, tell him what he needs to know."

"I suppose you're right," says Mael. He looks toward Niall, whose eyes rove over the ground around his feet. "Veleda wants to tell you something about dust."

Niall's head jerks up and his eyes meet his countryman's. Mael smiles, looks at Starkad, and nods. "Well, that proves it. Who else but Niall mac Llyr would show such an interest in dust?" He laughs and Starkad joins in. Puzzled, Niall shakes his head.

"Here are her words," says Mael, "and they'd better do something to help you or hinder you, because I've carried them all the way from Gaul, right through a bloody Saxon camp, to give them to you. Just like Veleda though, I'll warn you, they're not very easy to understand. She seems to think that everyone knows as much as she does.

"This is what she told me. The vessel is old but it is still sturdy. When you see it, it will be filled with dirt.

You will see others. Ask questions only when the exact vessel is set before you. If you succeed, come only to me. Take nothing to the wizard."

Niall stares at the Irishman, his eyes wide and his mouth drooping. The Dane laughs. "Well, that's got you," he says, and he looks at Mael, who smiles. "There's the proof we needed of who you are. It's plain you know what she's talking about, and since Mael and I couldn't figure it out, you must be the one it was intended for. That's why Mael's questioning was useless. If you knew, the surprise would be enough to give you away."

Niall shakes his head. "I don't know what she's talking about," he says. The Dane laughs again.

"Yes you do," he says. "At least, you know the most of it. The words themselves may be confusing. They always are. Veleda talks like that whenever she has something important to say. You may not understand now what she means, but before your mission is finished, you will. She meant to catch you, it seems, before you got too far along."

Mael cuts in. "And that's why I asked about the wizard. Plainly he knows something about this, and just as plainly Veleda wants him kept out of it. Do you know why that is, Niall?"

"No."

"Because she hates him. Or rather because he hates her. That became clear the last time we saw them together."

"Yes," says the giant. "But it's not as simple as Mael would like to believe. I don't think Veleda hates anyone, although she comes close with Merlin. Merlin hates her, that's sure, but why he hates her my stubborn friend here has no idea. I've tried to explain it to him and so has she, but he won't listen. An Irishman in love is without the power of thought."

"And what don't I know about it?" Mael asks, annoyed once again.

"Much. But that can wait. For now we must deal with our visitor here. He has heard Veleda's message, and it has affected him. It has filled him with questions we can't answer. Perhaps it has even upset his plans." He waits for Niall's response.

"It's not what the wizard told me," Niall says at last. "I'm going to have to choose."

"Choose?" Mael shouts. "Choose? Between what? The word of that bloody wizard and the warnings of Veleda? What, tell me, is there to choose?"

"Calm down," says the giant. "Merlin has told him one thing, Veleda another. He has seen Merlin and heard him speak. He knows nothing of Veleda except what Arthur and Merlin may have told him, which can't be very helpful."

"No," says Niall. "That's only part of it. I have reason to trust the wizard but none to trust your Veleda. At least one thing Merlin told me has been true, even though I was never sure I believed him. He may hate your woman, Mael mac Llyr, but he is far greater than you believe."

Mael stays quiet, the Dane's words holding him in check. Starkad asks, "What has he shown you to be true?"

"It doesn't matter," replies Niall after a long pause. "But there is something else, and I don't know how it fits the woman's message. She can't have known anything about it."

"Maybe not," says the Dane. "But she knows bloody

near everything else, so why not that? Whatever it is that's bothering you, let me tell you that things will get much worse. For Veleda to send both of us across Britain and into Ireland for no more important reason than to relay a message means that something important is going on. At least to her. I'm glad you're doing it and not me. The last time she was this concerned, my friend and I were almost killed by Merlin's damned wyvern. We destroyed it, but only with her help. If this is as serious, I want no part of it."

Niall has heard few of Starkad's words. "I must know," he says. "Can you get word back to her? Fast?"

Mael looks up. "Fast? How fast? We have other things to do here."

"A few days," Niall replies. "I don't know. I have no idea how long it will take me to find what I'm looking for."

"A few days?!" cries Mael. "By the gods to whom our people swear, Niall mac Llyr, if you think I've ridden right across the entire British island, fought my way onto the first boat to Ireland, and spent the last two days searching hill and valley for you when I could have been doing many things I consider more important, only to turn around and go back at full speed the same way I came, then you're even more of a fool than I thought when we met. From here I go north, not east." With that, he walks back to his horse.

"This is important," Niall says to Starkad. "Veleda can't know about this yet, and it might change her message. Will you go?"

"Not unless I must," replies the Dane. "I have

business in the north. With Mael. But if I must, what do you want me to tell Veleda?"

"Tell her . . ." Niall pauses, unsure whether Starkad should know. If Starkad tells Veleda, Niall argues with himself, Merlin may find out. If Merlin is right, and Veleda is wrong, the whole quest might fail. But if I don't . . . "Tell her I have spoken with the ghost of Uther Pendragon. Tell her he awaits a visit from Death."

Fear enters the giant's eyes, fear mixed with awe. "Uther Pendragon?" he whispers. "My God. Yes. I will tell her. Where will I find you?"

"On the western coast, searching for a castle owned by a fisherman." I didn't ask him, he thinks. I told him.

"North of the river?" Starkad asks.

"I don't know."

"No matter. I'll find you. Give me two days."

"I'll try."

Starkad walks to his horse and mounts. With Mael, he walks along the road and disappears over a near hill. Suddenly Niall hears shouting, then what seems to be fighting, and finally the sound of hooves galloping toward him. Over the hill rides the Dane, and when he sees Niall he raises his axe high above his head and rushes on.

Niall runs to the top of the hill, where he sees the figure of Mael mac Ronan lying motionless in the ditch on the road's eastern side. The horse grazes nearby.

Scooping cold mud from the ditch, Niall pours it over his countryman's face. At first nothing happens, but as the mud finds its way into his eyes Mael snorts, coughs, then sits up and shakes his head. Snarling, he wipes his eyes clean and opens them, then looks at Niall, throws back his head, and howls. "The bloody bastard!" he yells to the sky. "If I ever see that goddamned bloody bastard again I'll ram his god-damned bloody brainless head straight up his ass and make him eat shit."

Unable to help himself, Niall laughs. Plainly, Mael is not hurt, but just as plainly he will not appreciate being laughed at, and Niall backs away as he does so. Even so, the man in the ditch rises to his feet and steps towards him, his right hand on the hilt of his sword. Niall forces himself to stop laughing.

"Are you hurt?" he asks.

"I don't know yet, but you're about to be."

"Take it easy. I'm sorry I laughed. Why did he attack you?"

"Said he didn't need me anymore, and that he was going off on his own. I told him to stop being stupid, and we yelled for a while, but that's nothing new. But then he swung his damned axe at my head, and I fell off my horse trying to get out of the way. Then he jumped on me and pounded my head. I'm lucky I'm still alive. That bastard is strong."

"I don't think it was just luck," says Niall. "He probably had no reason to kill you."

"Starkad the Dane doesn't need a reason," Mael replies. "Do you have anything to do with this?"

"Probably, but I don't know what."

"Did he leave any wine?" Mael asks. Niall looks around and finds the Dane's sack lying in the grass beside the road.

"All of it, it looks like," he says to Mael.

Section 43

"Good. Give me some, and have some yourself. It's getting dark. We might as well drink what's here before we move on."

"Before *we* move on?" Niall asks.

"You're going north, aren't you? For a few miles at least? We might as well travel together, especially if we go at night."

"True," says Niall. "But what about the Dane?"

"Screw him," Mael shouts. "If he leaves his wine, somebody's going to drink it. This'll be the best wine I've ever tasted." He opens the flagon and sets to, gulp after noisy gulp. Temporarily sated, he hands the flagon to Niall, who drinks from it as well. "Now," Mael says, "that's better. I almost forgive the stupid bastard. Give me more, Irishman. I'm going to drink, and then I'm going to sleep it off. I'll probably burn with an aching head when I wake up, but right now I don't care." He takes the flagon and drinks again, then hands it back to Niall. Together, the two Irishmen drain the flagon and, against the trunks of two solid oaks, they fall fast asleep.

In the night Niall awakes. The moon is high, but is difficult to see in a sky filled with black clouds. Mael's horse stands sleeping just off the road, and Mael himself has fallen sideways away from his tree trunk. A wind blows sharply from the west, bringing with it the smells of salt and of rain.

Suddenly, far to the north along the road the two men are traveling, Niall hears the sound of a galloping horse. At first it is very faint, and he thinks he has imagined it, but with each passing second it grows louder and more distinct. Reaching out with his right hand, Niall shakes his companion. Mael mumbles something in his sleep, then, in an instant, grabs

Niall's arm and leaps to his feet, his hand already on his sword. When he sees it is Niall, he releases him.

"What do you want?" he asks. "Why did you wake me?"

Niall raises his finger to his lips and nods his head towards the north. "Listen," he whispers.

Now fully alert, Mael stands motionless and listens. Hearing the approaching horse, he looks at Niall and nods. He reaches for his shield, straps it onto his arm, and draws his sword. Before Niall can react, he steps toward the road.

"Wait," Niall whispers. "What are you doing?"

"Crossing the road," Mael whispers back. "I'll watch from there, you watch from here. That way, if anything happens, we'll come at them from both sides."

"But if we stay here and get your horse out of sight, nothing will happen."

"Maybe, but then we won't be able to stop them, either. I want to stop whoever it is."

"Why?" Niall asks. "What good will that do us?"

"I have my reasons," whispers Mael. "I told you I have other things to do in Ireland than just look for you. This may be the person I want."

Niall wants no part of this. "Then do it yourself, damn it. I have things to do as well, and I don't intend to get killed before I start. We don't even know who it is."

"True. But we do know it's only one horse, so it can't be more than two people. That many we can handle. Besides, if we capture their horse, you'll get to where you're going much sooner." Not waiting for Niall's reply, Mael sprints across the road.

The horse, Niall thinks. Mael's horse is still out in

Section 43

the open. He stands and runs to it, taking its halter and leading it into the trees. There he ties it to the lower branch of an oak. "Stay here," he whispers to it, "and don't make a sound."

Just as he finishes tethering the horse, he hears the sound of hooves approaching, nearer and nearer, louder and louder. It got here fast, he thinks, faster than I would have imagined. I'd best get back to the road. If Mael tries this on his own . . .

Before he reaches the road, Niall hears Mael's voice ring in the night. "Stop!" Mael shouts, his voice commanding and without fear. "Stop where you are. Stop or I will see to it that . . ."

Then, suddenly, as abruptly as it began, Mael's voice stops.

For a second all is silent. The west wind dies, and the face of the moon shows through the clouds. Peering through the trees Niall sees, outlined by the moonlight, a rider wearing a black cloak astride a black, shadowy horse. Facing him, standing in the road, stands Mael. Neither figure moves and neither speaks.

The horseman raises a whip above his head. Like a tongue of fire, the lash snakes through the night sky and licks the air in front of Mael's face. The crack jolts Niall's ears, and he sees Mael fall back. As if in answer to that crack, thunder assaults the night and lightning leaps in the sky, but no rain falls.

Mael picks himself up. He staggers backward along the road. The horseman raises his whip once more.

If Niall rushes in to help Mael, turn to section 48.

If he remains hidden, turn to section 46.

* **44** *

No, Niall thinks to himself. I need no curses, and perhaps I can find the goblet by myself. All curses are great risks, and there is no need to take such a risk. Not yet at least.

"I have decided," he says to the body. "I will go without knowing. There must be other ways."

Uther's eyes are closed. "You are wise, warrior, as are few men indeed. I give you only this, then. Find a castle in your homeland on an island near the western sea. The castle, it is said, is owned by a man who was once a fisherman. That is part of what I know."

Niall leaps up. "But doesn't even *that* knowledge curse me as you said it would?"

"It may be," says Uther Pendragon. "Now go. I will say no more." With that, the body lies silent.

Niall takes one last look around the tomb, then a sudden chill causes him to shudder and he steps quickly into the passageway.

Turn to section 41.

* **45** *

Tearing his eyes from the horseman once more, Niall grabs Mael's shoulders and pushes him toward the side of the road. Unexpectedly, because he seems completely out of himself, Mael resists. He looks at Niall but there is no hint of recognition in his eyes. Mael has not lost his strength, though, and for a

Section 46

moment he and Niall wrestle near the side of the road, with Mael's curses filling Niall's ears.

Then Niall hears the unearthly neigh of a horse, and he snaps his neck around to see the black steed shaking its head and beginning to prance. Must get Mael off the road, he thinks, before the horseman charges. I don't know what he is, but if he can do this to Mael mac Ronan, I wish never to find out. But Mael is strong and, even without alertness, he battles Niall to a stalemate.

Make a Strength roll (−5 modifier) for Niall. If it succeeds, Niall pushes Mael into the ditch and turns to face the horseman. Turn to section 50.

If the Strength roll fails, Niall must decide whether to keep trying to push Mael off the road or turn and face the horseman.

If he turns to face the horseman, turn to section 42.

If he continues to push Mael into the ditch, turn to section 53.

* 46 *

Again the whip cracks, and again Mael staggers back. The Irishman rises slowly to his feet once more, then stands and faces the black horseman. Finally Mael speaks, and Niall hears fear in his voice. "Go back!" he commands, but the command is filled with terror. Niall cannot see the horseman clearly, but Mael's voice tells him all he wants to know. It is horrible beyond words.

The horseman advances, his mount taking one long step along the road. Mael does not move, and Niall marvels at his courage. But when the horseman raises his whip anew, Mael seems to cringe. He backs away but the black horse follows. At last the whip sings in the sky, and Niall sees his countryman cover his eyes and fall to the ground. Mael's scream fills the night.

Suddenly Mael's horse whinnies, and the horseman turns his head toward Niall's side of the road. As the moon finds its way through the clouds, Niall sees the horseman's face, and at that sight he shudders and falls to the ground. Mastering himself, he struggles to his feet and runs towards Mael's horse. The trees whirl around him, and the horse sways as if in a heavy wind. Almost delirious, the Irishman manages to untie the horse and scramble onto his back. The horse needs no encouragement to run. As soon as he is free, he turns into the woods and gallops as hard as he can. He cares nothing for direction, nothing for the dangers; he wants only to disappear. Niall, clinging hard to his mane, can only sob and agree.

Turn to section 51.

* **47** *

"I want to know," says Niall slowly. "I must." He pauses, and when the body does not speak he asks, "Will you tell me as you promised?"

The body begins to lift itself from the slab. "You have decided. I cannot say your choice is wise, but neither can I say it is foolish. That judgment lies in the future." Uther Pendragon tries to rise, then falls back upon the slab. Niall moves to help him.

"No," says Uther, "do not help. I am beyond that. Listen, and do not move.

"Merlin and Arthur are right. The goblet they want is in your homeland. But this is no ordinary goblet, and you cannot steal it by ordinary means. Arthur's goblet—for he would have you believe it is his—rests on a table somewhere in the halls of an old Irish castle. The castle is near the sea, and its ruler is an old fisherman whose name is not known. None now living in your land claim to know of the fisherman, and because of that I was unable to find him. Arthur cannot know of the fisherman, and Merlin would surely have told you about him if he had known, so I believe I remain the only Briton aware of his existence. But they have at least guessed right, that only an Irishman will find a way to the goblet. Only an Irishman, Niall mac Llyr, can understand the Irish.

"If knowledge brings a curse, then you are now partly under that curse. But I know—or at least suspect—one thing more, and it is this! The fisherman's castle stands on an island, not on the mainland. That island is one filled with mystery, an ancient, desolate, rock-bound piece of land not far off the sea to the west. Find that island and you will find your goblet. But what happens then I do not know. I never made it that far.

"One thing more. It is said—though I do not know if it is true—that he who seeks the goblet must ask several questions along the way. Not all questions will further him in his quest, only those that do not directly ask about the goblet itself. To ask *about* the goblet, until it is in sight, is to lose it forever. So ask where you must and as often as you can, but never about the thing you seek."

Uther reaches his hand slowly toward Niall and then draws it back.

"Take my amulet, Irishman," Uther says. "It should help you if you make it to the fisherman's island. If you do not, and if you are still alive, return it to me. If you die, perhaps someone will bring it to me later." Niall walks to the slab and takes, from around Uther's neck, the polished stone and the chain to which it is tied. He puts the amulet around his own neck, then steps back toward the exit.

"And now, Niall mac Llyr," says Uther Pendragon, "my time is ended. It is time for my return. I wish you well."

The body of Uther Pendragon relaxes completely, as if it has just died anew. Silence covers the tomb. Niall rises and prepares to leave, but then he sees the man-bear stir on the floor. The red cloak flies from the monster as it pushes itself to its feet. Niall watches, all the while backing toward the exit.

The beast lumbers toward the stone slab. Niall's

Section 47

right hand clasps the hilt of his sword, but he silently prays that he will not have to fight. His prayers are unneeded. The man-bear heads straight for the slab, its arms stretched forward.

Suddenly, Uther Pendragon sits straight up. He turns toward the monster and begins to raise his hands to its face. But he is too late; the beast wraps its hands around Uther's head and starts to pull. Uther screams, and the sound assaults Niall's terrified ears.

The man-bear pulls harder, and Niall hears the sickening sound of a head being torn from its body. Long, long seconds pass, and still the sound goes on. Then, finally, the head comes off, and Niall waits for the silence.

It does not come. The head continues to scream, louder and harder and with increasing force. It deafens the Irishman, who now turns his unbelieving eyes away from the ghastly spectacle and leaps toward the exit. Into the passageway he runs, sweat pouring from his neck and face. When he stops to look behind him, he sees the man-bear settling to a sitting position in the middle of the tomb, Uther Pendragon's screaming head clutched in its hands. Niall turns and runs again.

Turn to section 41.

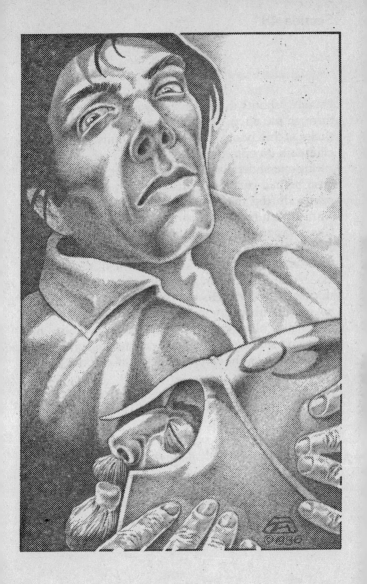

* **48** *

"Mael!" shouts Niall as he drags his leaden feet through the ditch. "I'm coming. Hold on." The mud sucks at his boots, but he draws himself free and clambers up onto the road.

But one short glance at the horseman makes him wish he had run the other way. Only a brief second passes during that look, but Niall stops, transfixed with sudden fear. Mustering all his will, he turns his face away from the horseman and back toward his countryman.

If the sight of the horseman terrified, the sight of Mael sickens. The man grimaces in pain, and his eyes shine with horror. His sword is raised but he makes no move with it nor does he seem to realize he is holding it. Niall sprints toward him, grabbing his arms and shaking him. Mael does not respond. Niall turns and sees the whip held high above the horseman's head.

If Niall draws his sword and faces the horseman, turn to section 42.

If he tries to push Mael off the road, turn to section 45.

If he races towards the horseman, turn to section 49.

* **49** *

Niall leaps toward the mounted figure, drawing his sword as he runs. The lash of the whip cracks above him, but he manages to avoid it. Suddenly the black horse rears, and Niall strikes at it. His sword passes through it.

Frightened and desperate, Niall raises his sword above his head and swings at the horse's rider. This time the sword strikes something, but it is not nearly the blow it should have been. The horse rears again, and Niall jumps aside to avoid its hooves. He sees the whip rise in the air once more, and he braces for its sting.

Roll for damage from Niall's sword on the horseman. Then turn to section 50 and continue the combat.

* **50** *

Use the combat rules to determine the winner. The horseman attacks with his whip only. He does not use the horse to kick, trample, or charge. No matter where Mael is, he does not enter the battle. Niall can damage the horseman only with his sword. He cannot damage the horse at all.

THE HORSEMAN
To hit Niall: 13   To be hit: 5   Hit points: 48
Damage with whip: 1 D6+4

The horseman gets one crack of the whip every two rounds beginning with the first round. If, in any round, the horseman obtains a damage result of 10 (rolls a 6), make a Dexterity roll. If it succeeds, Niall ducks under the whip and takes normal damage. If it fails, Niall is struck in the eyes. In that case, Niall must make a Constitution roll each round thereafter. If the Constitution roll succeeds, Niall fights normally for that round. If the roll fails in any round, turn to section 56.

If Niall defeats the horseman, turn to section 54.

If Niall is defeated, turn to section 29.

* 51 *

Niall and Starkad the Dane stand with their backs to the sea, high on a rock on Ireland's western coast. Niall has been searching a week for the fisherman's castle, but he cannot find it himself and nobody he meets seems to know where it is. He had begun to think about giving up when Starkad found him.

"The lance," urges Starkad. "Ask about the lance."

Niall shakes his head in puzzlement and disbelief. "What lance?" he asks. "Did she tell you that?"

"No," Starkad replies. "I told her about Uther Pendragon, and for a moment I honestly think she was stunned. Speechless. I've never seen her that way before. I liked it."

Niall nods, then says, "What did she say about Uther? Or did she say anything at all?"

"Quite a bit, but not much made sense. You must remember, I don't understand Veleda very often.

When I do, I worry because it usually means trouble —for Mael and me, at least."

"Did you understand any of it?" Niall asks.

"Some," the giant replies. "She is concerned, very much I think. She kept muttering something to herself, something about father and son, which I suppose was about Arthur and Uther. And then something about Merlin—she was really upset when I told her how Merlin got into the act."

"But what did she say about Merlin?"

"Nothing good, but she seemed to understand. 'Yes, it adds up,' she said a few times. Pendragon seemed to give her a great deal of information."

Niall nods again, then looks around him, deep in thought.

Finally he asks, "Anything else? Did she have any other advice except to ask about the lance? Any ideas about how to find this fisherman?"

"No," says Starkad. "That's all. But she plainly thought it very important. I think she's gone to deal with Merlin."

"Well, thanks, friend," says Niall. "I'm no closer to solving this puzzle than I was, but maybe Veleda's advice will be useful if I get that far."

The Dane walks away, then turns and says, "I'll go to Mael now. Do you know what the horseman was?"

"A Dullahan. Headless. Black. No Irishman needs to be told." He shivers. "It was horrible, Starkad. Watch the nights. They only show at night."

"Until I met Mael mac Ronan," Starkad replies, "I distrusted most of your Irish daydreams and stories. He taught me not to be too sure. But this . . . I don't know whether to believe in it or not."

"I can't help you there," says Niall. "I saw what I

saw. If you can help Mael, maybe he can tell you more."

Starkad turns away. Niall watches as he mounts his horse and takes the road to the east.

Mark an "M" in the Special Events box of Niall's character record. Then turn to section 55.

* **52** *

Niall ducks as the horseman's whip snaps over his head. Looking up, he sees the horseman raise the whip once again. When it snakes toward him, he drops to his stomach and rolls to his right. Leaping to his feet, he closes in at an angle to the mounted apparition and slashes at the horse's front leg. Quicker than any earthly beast, the horse wheels away before Niall's blow lands.

As the Irishman draws a breath, the horseman turns to face him once more. The night-black horse prances sideways as its dark rider raises his whip high above his head. Niall braces himself, his knees slightly bent. His timing, he knows, must be perfect.

It isn't. He leaps a split second late, and the whip rips into his left forearm. Hot-cold agony runs down Niall's arm into his fingers. Dropping his sword, Niall clutches his wound. The whip rises again.

This time Niall is ready. His left arm is still throbbing with more pain than a simple whip cut should cause, but when he sees the whip begin its descent, he dives to the ground beside his sword. As he grabs it, he rolls towards the horse, over and over, until he thinks he has rolled far enough. Up he leaps, and as he does so he sees the black horse rearing, its front legs poised to come down on his head. He feels the bite of the whip slash his neck as he leaps to the side once more.

The burning cold flows upward, filling Niall's head until he is certain that it will burst like an overripe melon. Almost by accident, his leap carries him to the horse's flank. Planting his feet, he swings his sword at the horseman's left leg. He feels it cut through the black cloth, then leaps back and watches in shock as black blood gushes from the wound. He closes with the rider once more, and this time his sword opens a wide gash near the horseman's hip. The rider tries to back away, whip ready to strike, but Niall continues to close and slash. The whip strikes his back, and once his left leg, but the cold-hot pain can no longer shock him and Niall presses on.

Finally, blood dripping into his eyes from a welt on his forehead, his left arm numb with pain, Niall strikes the decisive blow. Deep into the horseman's side his sword bites, and Niall pulls it out, releasing a gush of black blood.

Once more Niall raises his sword, and once more he swings it at the horseman's body. No sound, no scream, not even the slightest whisper comes from the horseman's mouth, but the lash of his whip grows weaker with each crack. Niall feels stronger with each slash of his sword. As the battle goes on, he knows again the excitement of impending victory. He will win. He knows that now.

Suddenly the shadowy horse rears, and the mighty hooves rest for a moment high above Niall's head. The Irishman glances up, raises his shield arm, and leaps backward out of the horse's path. The horse wheels in the road, and the black horseman rides northward into the night. In a mere second, he is gone.

Niall looks to his left and sees Mael lying face down on the road behind him. Kneeling beside him, he grasps Mael's shoulders and gently rolls him over. The sight startles him, and he closes his eyes and suppresses his urge to vomit.

The horseman's whip has opened deep cuts in Mael's face. Long gashes lie open and bleeding. The nose is crushed and its splinters show through the skin. Blood streams from the mouth, and teeth stick to the dried blood on the lips. But worse than all this, both eye sockets are filled with the pulpy remains of what were once Mael's eyes.

Niall rises and walks to the ditch. He scoops up a handful of cool, muddy water and begins to wash the cuts on Mael's face. Then, as if in sympathy, the rains come, huge drops at first, then a heavy fall, and finally unstopping sheets of driving water. Niall turns his companion's face into the storm and lets the mercy of the gods cleanse and heal it as they will. Exhausted and sick, Niall falls to the ground and sleeps.

When he awakes, the sky is clearing, the great gray clouds riding the wind toward the east. The sun shines on the two men, and Niall looks at Mael. His face is clean now and the bleeding has stopped. The sockets of the eyes are nearly empty.

Niall shakes his comrade. Mael grumbles, then turns and sits up. "I'm blind," he says, perhaps to Niall, perhaps to himself, perhaps to the wind. "I

Section 52

know," Niall says. "Come. We must get you some help."

"I'm blind, my friend," is all Mael says. "The Dullahan, he is the one who blinded me. The Dullahan. His whip. My eyes. I'm blind."

It goes on. Through the long hours of that day, Mael talks ceaselessly but never more articulately than that, and never about anything else. He never mentions Niall or Starkad or even Veleda. He talks only of his blindness. He is mad, Niall knows, and he needs help.

Finally the two men enter a small village. Among the huts only one wooden building stands, plain and austere in the setting sun. Niall and Mael enter and a priest comes forward from the front of the church to greet them.

Niall says nothing. He merely points and the priest listens to Mael's ranting. Nodding, the priest disappears through a door and returns with a thick brown robe. He places it around Mael's shoulders and nods again. This is the signal, Niall knows, for him to leave.

Turn to section 51.

* **53** *

Make another Strength roll. If it succeeds, Niall has pushed Mael into the ditch and turns to face the horseman. Turn to section 50.

If the Strength roll fails, read on.

Niall struggles but Mael is too strong to be moved. In terror, Niall makes one last, desperate, futile try.

Then he hears the horse. He looks up the road and sees the unearthly horseman charging toward them, his whip high above his head. Niall shakes himself loose from Mael's grip and reaches to draw his sword. He drops to the ground as the lash of the whip rings in his ears.

Suddenly, Mael steps in front of him and walks towards the horseman. "No!" shouts Niall, and he reaches for his companion. The horseman brings down his whip. At the crack, Mael cries out and covers his face. "My eyes!" he screams. "My eyes. My eyes. My eyes . . ."

Use the combat rules to determine the winner. The horseman attacks with a whip only. He does not use the horse to kick, trample, or charge. Mael does not enter the battle. Niall can damage the horseman only with his sword. He cannot damage the horse at all.

THE HORSEMAN
To hit Niall: 13   To be hit: 5   Hit points: 48
Damage with whip: 1 D6+4

Section 54

The horseman gets one crack of the whip every two rounds beginning with the first round. For the first round, make a Dexterity roll. If it succeeds, Niall fights normally this round. If it fails, the horseman gets an extra attack this round.

If, in any round, the horseman obtains a damage result of 10 (rolls a 6), make a Dexterity roll. If it succeeds, Niall ducks under the whip and takes normal damage. If it fails, Niall is struck in the eyes. In that case, Niall must make a Constitution roll each round thereafter. If the Constitution roll succeeds, Niall fights normally for that round. If the roll fails in any round, turn to section 56.

If Niall defeats the horseman, turn to section 52.

If Niall is defeated, turn to section 29.

* **54** *

Niall ducks as the horseman's whip snaps over his head. Looking up, he sees the horseman raise the whip once again. When it snakes toward him he drops to his stomach and rolls to his right. Leaping to his feet, he closes in at an angle to the mounted apparition and slashes at the horse's front leg. But quicker than any earthly beast, the horse wheels away before Niall's blow lands.

As the Irishman draws a breath, the horseman turns to face him once more. The night-black horse prances sideways as its dark rider raises his whip high above his head. Niall braces himself, his knees slightly bent. His timing, he knows, must be perfect.

It isn't. He leaps a split second late, and the whip rips into his left forearm. Hot-cold agony runs down Niall's arm into his fingers. Dropping his sword, Niall clutches his wound. The whip rises again.

This time Niall is ready. His left arm is still throbbing with more pain than a simple whip cut should cause, but when he sees the whip begin its descent, he dives to the ground beside his sword. As he grabs it, he rolls towards the horse, over and over, until he thinks he has rolled far enough. Up he leaps, and as he does so he sees the black horse rearing, its front legs poised to come down on his head. He feels the bite of the whip slash his neck as he leaps to the side once more.

The burning cold flows upward, filling Niall's head until he is certain that it will burst open like an overripe melon. Almost by accident, his leap carries him to the horse's flank. Planting his feet, he swings his sword at the horseman's left leg. He feels it cut through the black cloth, then leaps back and watches in shock as black blood gushes from the wound. He closes with the rider once more, and this time his sword opens a wide gash near the horseman's hip. The rider tries to back away, whip ready to strike, but Niall continues to close and slash. The whip strikes his back, and once his left leg, but the cold-hot pain can no longer shock him and Niall presses on.

Finally, blood dripping into his eyes from a welt on his forehead, his left arm numb with pain, Niall strikes the decisive blow. Deep into the horseman's side his sword bites, and Niall pulls it out, releasing a gush of black blood.

Once more Niall raises his sword, and once more he swings it at the horseman's body. No sound, no scream, not even the slightest whisper comes from the horseman's mouth, but the lash of his whip grows weaker with each crack. Niall feels stronger with each slash of his sword. As the battle goes on, he knows again the excitement of impending victory. He will win. He knows that now.

Suddenly the shadowy horse rears, and the mighty hooves rest for a moment high above Niall's head. The Irishman glances up, raises his shield arm, and leaps backward out of the horse's path. The horse wheels in the road, and the black horseman rides northward into the night. In a mere second, he is gone.

Thunder rolls in the distance. A bolt of lightning pales the night's blackness. The first drops of rain, huge and fresh, fall on Niall's face.

Then he hears Mael's voice: "DULLAHAN!" it shouts. "DULLAHAN!" Over and over it cries out that one word, and Niall kneels in the muddy road and covers his ears. The lightning grows brighter with each flash and the thunder louder with each burst. Niall gains control of himself, stands, and walks to his comrade. Mael lies on the ground shouting. "DULLAHAN!" The cry reverberates in Niall's brain.

He helps Mael to his feet. Wounded hardly at all but staring straight ahead into the rain, Mael follows willingly. Niall takes his arm and leads him away. Mael's horse has run off.

"Come on," Niall says. "We've got to get help."

"DULLAHAN!" comes the shout, and Niall looks anxiously down the road.

Hours later, the two men enter a small village. Among the huts only one wooden building stands, plain and austere in the setting sun. Niall and Mael enter, and a priest comes forward from the front of the church to greet them.

Niall says nothing. He merely points and the priest listens to Mael's shouts. Nodding, the priest disappears through a door and returns with a thick brown robe. He places it around Mael's shoulders and nods again. This is the signal, Niall knows, for him to leave.

Turn to section 51.

∗ **55** ∗

Niall stands on the steps of an ancient castle as a cold rain pelts down upon him. The door is plain—unadorned and without a knocker—and for a moment he does not know how to make those within aware of his presence. Then he notices a small wooden mallet resting in a stone basin attached to the wall just to the right of the door. Taking it in his hand, Niall hammers on the huge wooden door.

As he awaits a response, his mind takes in his bleak surroundings: a small island filled with old, gnarled trees and long, brown-green grass, rocks that slice through feet and holes that grasp ankles and snap legs. He thinks back on the trip to the island, and how he discovered it. A long journey, in days if not in miles, a journey that took him up and down Ireland's west coast, asking questions and searching every day until he dropped in exhaustion each evening.

He remembers the first days of his search, when all his questions met blank stares, when farmers and villagers alike regarded him suspiciously and offered him neither food nor lodging. Half a year has passed now, half a year of useless conversations, unanswered questions, and open hatred from the people he has met. For days at a time, he would go without eating because the search nagged at him until it became an obsession. Then, one day, he looked down into a pool of still water and saw a bearded, haggard, ghostly thin man looking back. When he moved, the thin man moved. When he jumped, the thin man jumped also. When he yelled, the man in the pool opened his mouth in a silent scream. He knew, of course, who it was but he refused to believe it.

Refused, that is, until the children began running from him, screaming as they ran and hurtling themselves into their mothers' arms. When that happened, the farmers, the villagers, the fishermen, even the priests began ordering him away. They were gentle with him at first, then commanding, and finally they used force to expel him. So he went, despairing of his mission and cursing Arthur, Merlin, and Uther Pendragon. He wanted desperately to give up, to go back to Britain and fight in Arthur's wars or to cross to Gaul, maybe even Rome or Byzantium, as far from this madness as possible.

But the mission drew him on, and the search for the castle became his reason for being alive.

And then one day, with yet another storm threatening the sky, he came to a old, ill-kept house somewhere between the latest village and the sea. No dogs guarded it and no children ran howling from him. No one emerged, butcher knife in hand, to order him off the land, and no window opened in the back to allow the inhabitants to escape. Nothing happened at all, and for Niall this was almost like a dream.

He walked through the long, tangled grass up to

the door and knocked. "Come in," said a woman's voice from within, and Niall pushed the door open.

The woman was lovely. She rocked on a chair in the middle of the room. Her black hair fell unbrushed far over her shoulders and her green robe, threadbare and tattered, hung almost to the floor. In her hands she held two long twigs. With them she seemed to be knitting even though she had no yarn.

"Come in, Niall mac Llyr," she said. "Close the door to keep out the rain."

He did so and at once he felt warm. He had noticed no smoke rising from the house and he saw no fire inside, but it was warm and smelled of cooked meat and the smoke of clean wood.

For a moment he stood silent as his hunger responded to the smell of the food and his clothes began to dry. Then he looked at the woman, and she smiled an achingly beautiful smile, her green eyes dancing, inviting Niall to be comfortable. Niall backed himself against the wall and slowly slid to a sitting position. The woman looked down at her work.

Suddenly what she had said registered within his numb brain, and he sprang to his feet. "You know my name!" he nearly shouted. "How do you know my name! I've never seen you before."

"That is true," said the woman. "And I have never seen you. But there are ways to know all things, if you choose to look for them. The secret is not in knowing, but in knowing what to know. Too many make the other mistake."

"That doesn't help," Niall replied. "I need no riddles. I've too many left unsolved."

The woman lay the twigs on the floor at her side. "I

am sorry," she said. "I do not mean to speak in riddles. But the languages of men leave few ways to say things and no way to say them properly. But I will try to be more clear."

She leaned back in her chair and began to rock. "I have been expecting you, Niall mac Llyr, because you have been looking for me for a long time. If you had found me when you first began, you might have surprised me, but by your third month of wandering I knew you were coming." Niall began to speak, but she motioned him to silence. "No," she said, "let me finish.

"There are ways of knowing. You must simply accept that for I will explain no further. But the Veleda cast the knowledge of your mission into the leaves of the trees, and the blades of the grass, even into the waters of the seas. I cannot do as much, but she can and she will when it is necessary. But neither she nor I, nor any of us, could will you here. You had to arrive in your own time and of your own volition. Do you understand?"

"I understand," replied Niall after some thought, "but I don't believe. Why should I?"

"Because I know your name. And I know that you have spoken with the dead king. That is enough."

"Who is this Veleda?" Niall asked, and waited anxiously for her answer.

Without hesitation the woman replied, "She leads me. She leads the few of us that remain. What power remains from the ancient days she carries with her. That is all."

Niall thought for several minutes before speaking again. Then he looked at the woman, and when she stared into his eyes his breath caught and his heart failed. His eyes closed and he fell to the floor. When they opened, she was tending to him, pouring a hot, bittersweet liquid into his mouth and swabbing the fever from his brow. Then, as he watched, she stood and opened her robe. She shrugged, and it fell to the floor in a swirl of green. Stepping from the robe, she returned to his side and began to move her hands over his body. Time stood still. Later, perhaps minutes, perhaps hours, her cool hand closed his eyes and he felt the pressure of her body atop him.

When he awoke she was knitting, and now there was yarn. He sat once more against the base of the wall. His stomach felt full and he was not thirsty. The rain still fell outside.

The woman raised her head. "Good," she said. "You have awakened. You have slept long." Rising, she said, "I will get food."

"No," said Niall. "I'm not hungry. But I thought . . ."

"Sleep brings many thoughts," the woman said. "Not all of them are true, but neither are all of them false. Whatever you choose will be true."

Niall stared at her, and this time her eyes, although they danced, had no other effect. "Who are you?" he asked at last.

"My name is Morrigan," she said after a slight pause. "I am one of the Veleda's women."

Niall nodded. He felt he understood. A witch, he thought to himself. She's a bloody witch. I knew that but I could not resist. He looked at her with disgust.

"I am sorry," she said. "I thought you knew."

"The name means nothing to me," Niall said, "but

my mission does. What can you tell me, and when can I leave?"

The woman shook her head. "When you came here you were hungry and thirsty and exhausted and wounded. I have changed all of that. Can you not be grateful?" She waits. "No, I suppose you cannot. The Veleda was correct."

"I don't give a damn about your Veleda, woman. I want the hell out of here. Now!"

"Of course. Let me tell you, then, that the fisherman's castle lies on an island off the western coast. Its name is ancient, but the coastal villagers call it Black Rock. It is directly west of here."

"And let me tell you, also, that if you return from that castle do not come back to this house. By then you will be under the Veleda's protection no longer. If you see me then, I will be the last person you will ever see. I promise you that, Niall mac Llyr, and I hate you."

With those words she looked into the Irishman's eyes and held them for several minutes. When she released him, he looked at her and saw that she was old and naked and so ugly that he tried to turn away. But again she caught his eyes, this time forcing him to look at her body, the skin hanging loosely, the shapeless breasts and legs now repelling all his senses. Finally she let him go, and he turned and ran from the house. When at last he turned and looked back, the house remained but the door was closed and no smoke rose from the chimney.

The rest, he now thinks, was easy. The villagers feared him and eagerly ordered their finest boatman to take him to the island they called Black Rock. The boatman did not talk to him, and Niall did not try to make conversation. Before they landed he saw the castle, bleak and dim in the setting sun. For one long night he camped, waiting for the sunrise. Now it has come.

Niall waits for an answer to his knock, then uses the mallet again. Still no response, and so a third knock. Finally he hears footsteps from within, and slowly the huge door opens. A young boy now stands before him.

"Hello," the boy says. "My grandfather asked me to greet you. Will you come in?"

Niall hesitates in surprise. "Don't you want to know my name? Won't your grandfather want to know who I am before you let me in?"

"I don't think so," replies the boy. "Grandfather didn't tell me to ask you. But my name is Mael. Does that help you?"

Laughing, Niall says, "Not really. I meant that you should ask *my* name. Since you haven't, though, I'll tell you. I'm Niall, and I've come to see your grandfather. At least, I think so. Is he the one who owns the castle?"

"Oh, yes," the boy says proudly. "All of it. I grew up in it. I know almost all of it by heart."

"That's good," says Niall, "because one day it will probably be yours." He knew enough not to ask about the boy's parents. He may never have known them. "Can you take me to your grandfather?"

"Of course," the boy responds, leading the way inside the castle. "That's what I'm supposed to do. Come on." He grabs Niall's hand, and the Irishman smiles as he follows.

The boy leads him through the entranceway, with walls of bare stone, through a door into a corridor that extends to both left and right for several feet before turning. In the wall to the left are three doors, but to the right there is only one. Past the door on the right walk Niall and Mael, the boy still holding his new friend's hand. Around the corner at the end of the corridor they stride, turning left down a longer cooridor with five doors along each side. Mael says nothing, but Niall can sense his pride in knowing his way around. "This is a big place," he says to the boy, and the boy smiles in reply.

When they reach the end of the corridor, they face a thick oaken door. The boy knocks and an old man's voice shouts, "Come in, my boy. Come in." The boy opens the door and pulls Niall inside. The old man sits with his back to them, writing at a large desk. His long white hair falls to his shoulders over a worn, brown robe. He rises and turns.

"Grandfather," says the boy. "This is Niall. He said I should ask who he is."

"Well done, Mael," says the old man. "I keep forgetting to tell you that." Then to Mael he says, "I'm sure you are hungry and tired. I will go now to make sure the meal is being prepared." Niall nods, and the old man reaches for an old cane. The boy runs to it and hands it to his grandfather. The old man smiles, rubs the boy's head, and hobbles out of the room. "Mael," he calls back, almost an afterthought, "make sure our guest is comfortable. I'll only be a few minutes."

"Come with me," young Mael says. "I'll take you to your room."

"My room?" Niall asks, completely taken by surprise. "What room? You didn't even know I was coming."

"That doesn't matter," says the boy. "You still need a room to sleep in. Any visitor here gets a place to sleep. Grandfather says that's the way it should be."

"He's right, little friend," Niall says. "I'm just not used to it. Most people I've met tell me to go away."

"They must be bad," the boy replies.

Niall laughs. "No," he says. "Not most of them. They're just scared, that's all."

Together they walk back down the corridor. Mael opens one of the doors they passed before, and Niall walks into his room. He asks the boy to leave the door open. Then he tests the bed, and it is soft. He strips off his shield and his boots and lies down. He is comfortable, as the old man wished.

He comes fully awake in seconds to a knock on his door. The boy, Mael, is standing in the corridor, hands on hips, patiently waiting for Niall to pull himself together.

"Hello, Niall," he says after a few minutes. "Grandfather asked me to wake you up. It's time for dinner."

"So soon?" Niall mumbles. "I must have fallen asleep."

"I know," says the boy. "I came by a couple of times. There's a basin of water beside your bed. I'll wait for you."

Niall splashes water on his face, drinking it as he does so. It is cold but tastes faintly of the sea. Then he rises and strides towards Mael.

"Wait," says Mael. "Grandfather says that you should change into the robe that's on your bed. It'll be much more comfortable, and it's clean, too."

Niall laughs. He hadn't been aware of how dirty he was, but Mael's remark made him think. "Thanks, little friend," he says. "It's been a while since I had a proper bath."

"You can have one after dinner. There isn't any time now. Dinner's ready, and fish isn't very good when it gets cold. Let's hurry."

The two walk together down the corridor, past the old man's study and past a large sitting room. When they come to a large oaken double door, Mael walks through it and Niall follows. They enter a room which is, without doubt, the most ornate room he has ever seen. Tapestries line the walls, all of them beautiful and some extremely detailed. On the rear wall is a large fireplace, alive now with the crackle of a hot fire. An oaken table dominates the center of the room. It is not large but is decorated in gold. The table is set with stone dishes, and steam rises from bowls of food. The smell of fresh cooked fish fills the air.

"Ah, come in. Come in," says the fisherman. He points toward a chair on the opposite side of the table. "This spot is yours, Niall. Our guests sit here always. Has Mael treated you well?"

"Certainly, sir. Better than I've been treated in many years, and I am grateful for that." He pauses. "May I ask your name?"

"Of course you may. I usually forget to give it. I am Mael." He laughs at Niall's disbelieving look. "Yes. The same name as my grandson. But you're Irish. You know how these things work. My son too was named Mael."

"I know of a Mael," Niall says. "Is he the same?"

"No," says the old man. "My son died six years ago.

He drowned while fishing. But we can talk of that later."

"My pardon, sir," Niall says. "We needn't speak of it at all. It just seemed a coincidence." He looks at the table. "If the dinner tastes a portion as good as it looks and smells, I will consider this my finest feast in many years. This is a welcome wholly unlooked for."

They sit, and a young woman serves the meal. There are potatoes, fresh bread with honey, cheese, and fish of many kinds. A cold soup waits in the bowls beside their plates, and cold, clear water fills the cups. Niall eats his fill, and when he is offered more he does not refuse. By the time he has finished, he is more than satisfied; he feels like a stuffed pig. Following his host's lead, he belches his approval. The old man smiles and the young boy laughs.

But there is more food to follow. Cakes and fresh fruit, a sweet, sticky pudding, and bread that is soft to the touch and sweet to the taste. Niall eats well again, then picks at the rest, but finally must stop on the point of bursting. He looks at the old man, then at the mess near his plate, and feels a twinge of embarrassment.

The two Maels look at one another and laugh again. The old man says, "And now, grandson, it's off to bed for you. Brenwin will tuck you into bed, and don't forget to pray. God bless."

"Grandpa!" he shouts. "But we've got a visitor. And maybe he can tell stories. You know how I love . . ."

"Mael! Nothing more about stories. Our guest is tired and now he is full. Let him rest. If he stays with us tomorrow, and if he wants to, he can tell you stories then. Now to bed."

Niall interrupts. "Little friend, your grandfather is

right. I feel too much at peace and still too tired to tell stories tonight. I must be wider awake to tell them well at all. But I do have stories to tell, and I promise you that I will tell them tomorrow if your grandfather invites me to stay. It's the least I can do for someone who has served me so well. So go to bed now, because tomorrow I'll keep you up late. Some of my stories will scare you so bad you won't sleep anyway."

"Really?" the boy exclaims. "Scary stories? Are they true?"

"Yes," says Niall. "Most of them are, but I wish they weren't. Scary stories aren't fun when you're part of them. They take too much work, and when they're all done they hurt."

"But you'll tell them? Just like they happened?" The young boy is nearly coming apart with excitement.

"Yes," says Niall, smiling. "I promise. Even the bad parts, even the parts where the heroes lose. It's sad when that happens, but sometimes it makes a great story."

"Grandpa, did you hear? Real stories?"

The old man nods and laughs. "Yes, Mael. And if you don't mind, I'll listen too, even though I don't like stories as much as I used to. Now—and I say this for the last time—get to bed."

Mael runs out of the double doors. The young woman tries to catch him. From down the hall Niall hears the boy's voice shouting, "Brennie, the man's going to tell me stories! Real stories, not made up stories!" Brenwin groans.

"That was well done," says the old man, "and it was also kind. Now I ask you formally. Will you stay, at least until tomorrow? Mael needs stories, and he gets too few of them."

Niall hesitates, then says, "It will be my honor to stay, my friend, and to tell your grandson my stories. I promise I will scare him as little as I can."

Laughing, the old man says, "Don't worry about it. He could use a good fright. Nothing scares him."

"Still," says Niall, "these might scare him too much."

The two men sit quietly for a time, the old man lost in the depths of thought and Niall in the pains of gluttony. Then Mael rises and, with a grimace, reaches for his cane. It is just beyond his fingertips. Niall gets to his feet, takes the cane, and hands it to his host. The old man nods in acceptance and appreciation, then hobbles, almost staggering, over to a chair near the fire. Niall looks at him with concern, wanting to ask about his leg, but hesitates. He has already brought up an unpleasant subject, the death of the boy's father, and he does not know if he should broach another. The old man grimaces as he sits.

If Niall asks the old man about his leg, turn to section 59.

If he does not ask, turn to section 57.

* **56** *

Pain tears through him as Niall blinks again and again, trying to clear his stinging eyes. As Niall's sight fades, the horseman becomes a dark blur. At last, Niall cannot see him at all. And then the night itself fails, and Niall forces open his eyes.

"I can't see!" he shouts, and he falls to the ground. Toward him comes the sound of hooves. Niall hugs the ground and feels a cold wind pass over him. The hooves gallop away to the south, and Niall lies on the ground, tears falling from his sobbing eyes.

Turn to section 29.

* **57** *

After a period of silence, the old man speaks again. He tells of the beginning of his castle, and of how it was built from plans he stole from a Roman official who was later imprisoned for losing them. He speaks of his son's fishing accident, of how he disappeared one day while at sea, and of how the only witness to the tragedy will not speak of it to this day. He speaks of sea monsters and of the half-dragon wurrum that he swears he saw only a few years ago, a half-eaten man dripping from its jaws. As the evening grows older, he tells of his dealings with the Druid priests and of his near-sacrificial death at their hands. Finally, he speaks of meeting Paedric himself. "Strong and

furious he was, my friend, and yet his eyes sparkled with laughter. Strange that the priests who now call him saint warn against all three: strength and fury and humor. All they know is solemn, and solemn is always dull." With that he lifts his head and laughs, but Niall does not understand why.

Finally old Mael struggles to his feet, takes his cane, and limps back to the table, motioning for Niall to join him. The Irishman stands, shakes his head to clear away the heat and the fatigue, then walks to the table and sits down. The old man looks at him.

"This, friend Niall, is my favorite time of the evening. Now we bring out the finest wine I have been able to find and we sit in silence and drink it while we listen to the fire and the sea outside. With this wine Brenwin will serve fresh sweetbread which you can spread with butter or dip in the wine as you wish. You aren't hungry, you say? No matter; eat and drink as little or as much as you want.

"But I must caution you. As we sit and enjoy our little snack you will hear sounds that you may never have heard before. Most are caused by the wind, but others are from the living things that inhabit the sea. Many creatures dwell there, and not all of them want this castle to exist. Some weep and complain and threaten, night after night after night.

"Still other sounds will be pleasant, for some of the creatures welcome men to their shores. Even these though can sound strange and even frightening. All I ask is for you to listen and not to talk, to allow the sounds to build. In the end you will stop distinguishing between the sounds and will hear instead one sound. It will remind you of waves crashing on a rock. That will be the sound of the living sea.

"Remember," he concludes, "make no sound yourself."

Brenwin enters the room bearing a large wooden tray, round and intricately ornate, filled with bowls and cups. The cups are silver and they show no markings. The bowls are wooden but they are ornate like the tray. Inside Niall's bowl is carved the symbol of a cross, a long spear sticking in its side. He looks at it questioningly but remembers Mael's request and says nothing.

The woman then takes a large wooden bowl from the tray and sets it on the table. From it wafts the smell of freshly baked loaves, and the scent is at once luxurious and sweet. Niall has thought himself full, but now he can barely wait to eat. Another bowl contains more bread, this smelling less sweat but more nourishing, and a large mound of freshly churned butter rests in a third bowl. Niall waits for Mael to begin.

"The bread cannot be eaten till it cools," says his host. "Quiet, now, and listen."

But for the fire, all is quiet. He hears the flames snap, he sees the bursts, and he hears the sound of air in the chimney. When the fire is quiet, Niall begins to hear the sea. Softly now, but building slowly, in a mounting crescendo of music and noise, it take shape in his mind. He closes his eyes and sees the waves and hears their splash as they wash the rocks outside the castle.

The sounds grow louder and harsher. The fire cracks sharply, and the waves pound the shoreline. Other sounds, soft at first but soon distinct, come to him. Some are filled with fear, other with hatred, others with glory. A battle, Niall thinks. A battle in

Section 58

the sea. Louder it grows, more furious, more impatient, with sounds of anger and terror and the cries of rally and of retreat and explosions like thunder and moans like the waking of the dead. It rolls, ever larger, ever more insistent, until the sounds become indistinct as if all combatants have merged into one. And now it sweeps through Niall's ears and crashes against his brain. For a second he sees only blackness and feels only cold.

Then he looks at Mael. The old man sits calmly, staring blankly at the fire. In his hand he grasps a long lance, longer than a Pictish spear, and from the lance's tip huge drops of blood drip to the floor.

If Niall honors his host's request for silence, turn to section 64.

If he asks about the lance, turn to section 58.

* 58 *

Niall watches for a minute more. The lance continues to drip blood, and the drops grow thicker. He longs to ask about it, to find out if it is real, but he respects his host's request—perhaps his command—for silence. Finally, spurred on perhaps by the strangeness of the room, perhaps by memories he only half-knows, he can resist no longer.

"The lance, Mael? What is this lance?" His whispered question echoes in the silence of the room.

Mael smiles. "At last, he says. At last." Standing, he grasps the lance in his right hand and hands it to Niall. "Throw it, Irishman, throw it into the flames."

A mixture of fury and excitement burns in the old man's eyes. Niall takes the lance.

If Niall throws the lance into the fire, turn to section 60.

If he hands it back to his host, turn to section 66.

* **59** *

"It is a long story," says the old man, "and no man should have to hear all of it. But since you have asked, something that no other visitor has done, I can tell you enough to satisfy you. Come, sit by me." He points.

Niall takes his place in a chair near Mael's. The two men sit in front of the fire, which cracks like a whip behind them. The flames are hot, and Niall's back warms through.

"Many years ago, well before you were born, my good guest, I was an important man. This castle then was a stronghold, and in it lived men and women of all ages, nobles and slaves alike. But I was hot-blooded in those days, and with my nobles I liked to go to war. From this island we would sail and row in ships by the dozen, guarding the Irish coast and traveling northeast to pillage the Picts. What a good time we had of it then, Niall, with the strong, pale-skinned women of dead Pict warriors living to fulfill our every command. We ate, we wenched, we drank. Oh, how we drank!

"But my hot blood at last stopped me. I fell in love with one of those Pict women, or at least I thought then it was love. I still do, perhaps. One night I

Section 59

returned after a raid, my armor spattered with Pict-ish blood, and in the camp were at least two dozen Pict soldiers burning our tents and looting what they could. And they were raping our women, our Pictish slaves that we had won for our own. They would rape them, women of their own race, and slice open their bellies. While they writhed in torment, the warriors would kick them, and piss on them, and cover them with shit. Then they would leave and move on to another slave who was being held by one of their goddamned soldiers.

"For a while I watched, because there were too many to attack and I was alone. But then I turned away, and I went into the woods, and I sobbed and I puked. I had seen no sign of my woman, but I carried no hope that she escaped. I wept long, but the weeping did little to stop my hatred.

"Then I plotted revenge. The noise from the camp was subsiding which meant, as it always means, that the soldiers were drunk and asleep, and all their enemies were dead. I crept silently toward the burnt remains of my tent, crawling through a host of dead slaves and sleeping Picts. Whenever I passed a Pict, I took his knife from his belt—all Picts carried a knife—and drove it into his throat. None of them even murmured. They were drunk beyond con-sciousness, and killing them was only too easy.

"I killed them all that way, all except the leader. For him I had a different plan. When I finally reached him, he and I alone were the only living beings in the camp. The thought of torture—torture to revenge my friends and my woman—came to me easily. With his own knife I carefully cut open his pants. Then, as soon as he shifted in his sleep, I cut out his balls.

"He screamed with the pain, and he tried to sit up, but I was on his throat before he could move. With one hand I clamped his throat and with the other I carved open his chest and his stomach. The blood flowed free and the guts sprang out, but he still lived. I stood and walked away, leaving him to die in his screams.

"I wandered through the camp the rest of the night, seeing in the moonlight the half-dissected corpses of our women and our men. They hadn't stopped with the women, I saw; they had desecrated the men as well. And then I saw my slave, my Pictish woman whom I loved beyond all reason. The sight of the others had been horrible, but the sight of her body was hell itself. I puked again, then sank to the ground at her side and cried.

"I heard a sound, and when I looked up I saw the Pictish leader standing before me. He had not died. He carried his guts in one hand, but they spilled where he could not hold them and fell halfway to the ground. In his right hand he held a mace, something he had picked off one of my soldiers, and this he raised above his head. I should have ducked, I should have rolled to one side, but my astonishment at the sight of him was too great. He dropped his guts to the ground, lifted the mace above his head with both hands, and brought it down on my leg. I felt the bone shatter and the blood spurt out, but in the pain I saw no more.

"When I awoke, the leader lay dead at my feet and my woman lay dead at my side. I tried to move but my leg was useless. Finally I dragged myself away. As I went I stole a Pict shield, the kind with the spike in the middle, and a Pictish tunic and cloak. My own clothes were soaked in blood and I did not care to wear them. Then I went in search of a Pict horse—these were cavalry to judge by their dress—and when I found one I rode back to my ship. There to greet me were my guards, who told me of beating back a Pictish raid. I told them nothing of what I had seen, but boarded my ship and ordered it back to the castle. I was ill for many weeks."

The old man falls silent, and Niall stares straight ahead. His stomach churns at the image of the mutilated corpses and the Pict leader, and he asks no questions. The fire is now lower.

Mark a "W" in the Special Events box of Niall's character record. Then turn to section 57.

* **60** *

Niall raises the lance to his shoulder and tests its balance. Then, in one swift motion, he draws his arm back and throws it into the fire, which embraces it by bursting into a red flare of flame. Niall covers his eyes against the glare.

The old man laughs, then looks at Niall and says, "Thank you, visitor. From the depths of my soul, thank you."

"For what?" Niall asks, bewildered and still shocked.

"Alone of all the guests I have had at this table, you are only the fourth to see the lance and the first to ask about it. Until you asked, I didn't know if you had seen it, but I hoped. When you asked what it was, I rejoiced."

"Why?" The explanation, so far, is unhelpful.

"Because the asking rids me of it. That is its curse, although curse is not the right word, only the closest. Someone had to ask about it. Until that happened, though, I was sworn not to tell anyone of it or the curse would have lasted forever."

Niall is still confused. "What curse? What did the curse do? Who placed it? And why on you?" More questions spring to mind, but he stops here.

"Patience, my good friend. One question at a time. In a sense, though, you've asked only one question, about the curse itself. I will explain what I might.

"You have heard the sound of the sea, have you not?" Niall nods. "And the sound of battle?" Another nod. "I told you earlier that not all things in the sea welcome my presence here. That is true. And I told you as well that my son was killed by something nobody saw. That is false. I saw it. It was a wurrum."

Niall nods, but still only half believes. As a child he listened to stories about these half-dragons, half-fish, and he even lay awake in terror at nights at the thought of them, but as an adult he has had no reason to believe they exist. Here now is a reason, but he is still uncertain.

"I was with my son," Mael continues. "We were only a short way off the coast, night fishing because the day catches were poor. Suddenly we saw an enormous tail fin break the surface, and then, several feet in front of it, the head of a serpent. 'By the gods to whom we pray, father,' said my son, 'a wurrum. A wurrum!' As quickly as we could, we turned our boat and rowed hard, but of course we weren't fast enough. The wurrum began to splash and writhe, and we were soon in danger of capsizing. My son

Section 60

carried a lance in the boat, stolen during a raid on the Picts, and he raised it and threw. It pierced the creature's right eye and drove itself deep into its brain. The creature wailed and screamed and thrashed more in its agony. The boat capsized and I went deep underwater. When I surfaced, my son was in the monster's jaws. I reached for the lance, extracted it from the right eye and drove it into the left, then drew it back out, ready to strike again. The monster writhed once more, then was silent. Mael, my son, was half eaten when the wurrum died.

"But the lance was cursed, probably because it entered the wurrum's brain. Whatever tiny powers of thought the creature possessed, it could curse even if it could not talk. The curse was this: for as long as the lance existed, my son would writhe, half eaten, in the monster's enormous jaws. But I could not destroy the lance myself. Someone else had to do it. I could relinquish the lance only if another person asked about it. That's why you had to throw it into the fire.

"Now it is gone. My son can sleep at last. But I warn you, my friend. The danger in breaking silence still exists. Do not ask about everything that happens here. Other questions may draw less happy answers."

Mark an "L" in the Special Events box on Niall's character record. Then turn to section 64.

* **61** *

Building up his courage, Niall opens his mouth to speak. But pieces of bread still stick to his palate, so he closes his mouth and works them loose with his tongue. Finally, his mouth clean, he prepares to speak.

"What . . . ?" he asks, and his voice almost shouts in the quiet room. "How are these loaves made?"

Mael looks up, takes a sip from his cup, and yells. "Brenwin," he shouts. "Come in here."

The woman enters, wiping her hands on a cloth. Mael motions her to the table. "Our guest," he begins, "wants to know how you make the loaves."

"A pleasure, sir," she says. "Which loaves?"

Niall points to the bowl with the grainy loaves. "These. They seem so unusual. With a strange—but excellent—taste."

Brenwin smiles. "Thank you. They are difficult to make, but there is nothing really unusual in them. The grain is oats, which does not grow here but which we get from Pict traders that land in the village on the shore. I add potato to give the loaves firmness. The taste you think is unusual is molasses. Its thickness rounds out the bread, and it combines with the oats to give the dark brown color. Then there are the usual ingredients: eggs, and yeast, of course, and honey. Do you want the precise measurements for each ingredient?"

"No," Niall replies, shaking his head slowly from side to side. "Thank you, but I think that's all I need to know."

Section 62

Brenwin smiles and leaves the room. Niall, now possessed of a new bread recipe to try out on Arthur and the Companions, looks sheepishly at his host.

Mael laughs.

Turn to section 69.

✳ **62** ✳

"The boy?" gasps Niall, his head swimming and pounding. "Why is the boy here?" The words are whispers, but the old man hears them. Niall's head drops to the table.

"Boy?" asks the fisherman, his calm voice dissolving the clouds in Niall's brain. "What boy? There is no boy here."

Niall looks up, and the room has stopped spinning. Only he and the old man sit at the table, but the old man now wears a gray cloak. Niall stares at it.

"Brenwin brought in some more wine, and I asked her for the cloak. I feel cold tonight. Have some more wine."

"No," says Niall, shaking his head clear. "How was she dressed?" Was all this just drunken delusion?

"She had her nightrobe on. Why?"

"Was it white?"

"Yes, but it must be cleaned. She has little time to look after herself. She brought more loaves as well. Do you want some? Or are you full?" The old man chuckles.

Niall turns his head away. "Sleep," he says. "All I want is sleep. Do you mind if I go to my room now?"

"Not at all," says the old man, taking a sip from his

cup. "It is ready, and you will not be disturbed. Call for Brenwin if you need anything during the night, but allow her some time to arrive. She sleeps heavily."

Niall nods, stands up, and walks, swaying, through the double doors. He gropes his way down the corridor, hoping he remembers the way to his room. At last he reaches it and falls on the bed fully clothed to fall asleep at once.

Turn to section 70.

* **63** *

Use the combat rules to determine who wins the fight.

MORRIGAN
To hit Niall: 7   To be hit: 13   Hit points: 12
Damage with knife: 1 D6+1; damage with magic: 2 D6

Because Morrigan's back is turned, she gets no attack the first round. Morrigan can only use her magic when she has time to concentrate. Therefore, she attacks magically only in rounds following a failed attack by Niall.

If Niall wins, turn to section 71.

If he loses, turn to section 29.

* **64** *

For a time the two men sit in silence. The fire brightens and warms the room, and the sound of the ocean seems to rock the room like a ship.

At last Brenwin appears, this time with a silver pitcher. She takes Niall's cup and fills it with clear wine, then does the same with Mael's. Setting the pitcher on the table, she nods to the old man. "Thank you," he says, and she leaves the room.

"The breads are cool enough now, and the wine is served. Now we can eat as we listen."

Suddenly extremely hungry, Niall practically grabs one of the sweet-smelling loaves. Breaking it, he spreads it thick with butter and devours it in four large bites. It is bread, yes, but it is unbelievably delicious: sweet, fresh, and very fine. He opens his mouth to speak, but Mael holds a finger to his lips. Nodding, Niall reaches for his cup and tastes the wine. It is cold and dry, and it warms his throat as it washes down the bread. Quickly Niall breaks a second small loaf, and just as quickly he devours it as well. Again he washes it down with the wine.

By contrast, Mael chews slowly. He is less than halfway through his first loaf by the time Niall finishes his second. Niall watches Mael drink and sees him sip rather than gulp. The fool, he thinks. If he doesn't hurry, I'll eat all the loaves. Whatever Niall once knew of elegance he has lost in his dealings with Arthur and the Companions.

After his second loaf, Niall feels a little less ravenous, and he decides to try the other bowl of loaves.

These are coarser, and they feel grainy, but still they smell superb. Breaking one of them, Niall spreads it with butter and takes a bite. Less sweet, he thinks to himself, but no less good. But there's something strange about it. Something cloying. With his tongue, he digs what he has chewed from between his teeth. The first type of loaf was exquisite, but these are more unusual. Perhaps, he thinks, I should ask what these are made of. Once again he feels pressed by curiosity.

If Niall breaks silence and asks Mael about the loaves, turn to section 61.

If he maintains silence, turn to section 69.

* **65** *

The boy smiles at the old man, who nods and pours from the pitcher into his grandson's small cup. The younger Mael lifts the cup to his lips, then licks them as he puts it down. Niall watches, his head beginning to clear, as the man and the boy exchange what seems to be a series of unspoken messages, with their eyes, their lips, their hands, even their eyebrows. They have a language, he thinks, that I don't even understand.

Brenwin has gone, closing the double doors behind her. The fire is no longer as hot, but now gives off a steady heat and noise. Niall watches as the boy spreads butter and honey on a loaf of sweet bread, then eats quickly and with obvious enjoyment. The boy drinks again, motioning for Niall to do the same.

Section 65

When Niall refuses, the boy just smiles and nods. The old man brings his cup to his lips and drinks slowly.

Still Niall's head has not fully cleared. It seems, in fact, to be getting worse. A dull throb has begun just above his eyes, a throb that intensifies with each crack from the fire. He shakes his head, but the fog refuses to lift. Once again he lowers his head to the table and closes his eyes.

As if in a dream, he hears a soft voice singing. When he raises his head, he turns his eyes to the double door and sees Brenwin entering, her white gown flowing to the floor and a golden tray in her arms. She sings as she walks, an ancient song that Niall knows but does not understand. A song of his people, he thinks, a song he should remember. To the table she walks, and on it she sets the golden tray.

On the tray, Niall sees now, are three tall goblets. One is of gleaming gold, its sides engraved with the image of a sprawling oak. The second appears to be gold, but dust covers whatever designs are carved upon it. The third, too, is golden, but this one is filled with dust. A red glow emanates from inside all three.

Brenwin takes the goblets from the tray and gently places them on the table. Then she fills Niall's cup with wine, but the wine now looks red. Niall shakes his head once more, then looks into his cup. It is red, he thinks. How can that be? The old man and the boy have not moved. The boy continues to eat, and the elder Mael continues to watch. Again the two Maels share unspoken words, their eyes dancing as they smile at one another. Brenwin smiles, too, as the music of her song fades into the sound of the fire.

Filled with the heat of the fire, the maddening familiarity of Brenwin's song, the strangeness of the

©1986

change in the wine's color, and now the mystery of the three goblets, Niall's head pounds as if it might burst. He hides it in his hands, running his fingers through his hair and shutting his eyes tight. He shakes his head, over and over, and presses it hard between his forearms. But still nothing clears. All he knows is a demand, an insatiable urge, an unstoppable desire to open his mouth and speak. If he breaks silence, if he asks the questions that form now in his brain, only then might his head know peace.

If Niall asks about the wine, turn to section 77.

If he asks about the goblets, turn to section 81.

If he asks about the song, turn to section 78.

If he resists the pressure on his brain, and holds his silence, turn to section 70.

* **66** *

The old man shakes his head, then takes the lance from Niall's hand and picks up his cane. Slowly he hobbles out of the room. In less than a minute he is back. He takes his place at the table once more.

Turn to section 64.

* **67** *

Forcing himself to turn away, Niall heads back into the forest. He lies down again, but he cannot sleep. The moon is now low in the sky, and soon the light of dawn appears through the trees.

Turn to section 75.

* **68** *

It is nearly midnight when Niall reaches the camp. Cold, tired and hungry, the weary horseman rides to within two hundred yards of the first tent before he is noticed. Then a shout: "A horseman!" and Niall hears the sound of scurrying feet. Shadows run to and fro amid the torches.

"Who are you?" shouts a gravel voice. "Speak."

"I am looking for the camp of Arthur the king," Niall replies. "I am returning to him."

"This is his camp," returns the voice, "but he is sleeping, and no one will disturb him."

"Oh, I don't want to disturb him," says Niall. "I'll wait till morning. Can I get food and a place to sleep? I have come a long way."

The voice is quiet for a time. Then it speaks. "Come with me," it says. "Tonight you will stay with me. If you are not one of Arthur's men, in the morning you will die anyway."

Niall rides towards him. When he sees the man

who has been speaking, he laughs. "Lancelot!" he exclaims. "It will be my pleasure to stay with you tonight."

At the sound of his name, Lancelot starts. As the Irishman draws nearer, into the light of the torches, the Companion shakes his head slowly. "Niall mac Llyr. You are foolish, Irishman. Unless you have come back with what Arthur wants, you are not welcome here. From me you get no welcome at any time." He pauses. "But I have made an offer," he says, "and I cannot lay it aside. Tonight you will stay with me, but in the morning we go to see the Leader as soon as it is light."

"How do I know you won't kill me in my sleep?" Niall asks, a half grin on his face.

Lancelot growls. "You know the answer to that, Irishman." He leads Niall through the camp.

In the morning Lancelot awakens him, and together they walk to Arthur's tent. Inside, the Leader sits on the floor, his sword across his legs, and Merlin the wizard sits to his right. Arthur nods to Niall and he waves Lancelot away. The Companion frowns but he obeys.

"You have returned, Niall mac Llyr," Arthur says. "Where is my goblet?"

"I don't have it," Niall says, looking the king in the eye.

Arthur's eyes open wide. "You don't have it?" He pauses, then adds, "And you return to me anyway? What kind of fool are you, man?"

"Not a fool at all," the Irishman replies. "I did what I could, but the goblet was not to be found. I have come back not to bring you your treasure, but to ask leave to be free to live in your lands or to return to my own and be assured you will not hunt me down."

Arthur laughs. "This, Merlin," he says, "is a strange man. He fails at what I ask of him, and then he returns to ask that I do not punish him. What do you make of that?"

Merlin stares at the floor as he speaks. "Only that he is honest, my lord, and that perhaps if he did not succeed no man could have. Perhaps the task was impossible."

"Have you grown soft, wizard?" Arthur asks, his voice rising in anger. "If I let every man live who failed me, how long would it take to destroy everything we've made so far? How long would I be alive? You would let this man go free?"

"I see no harm," Merlin replies. "If he is honest enough to return to you reporting failure, he will be honest enough to hold his tongue about your clemency. Perhaps you can put him to work another way, to atone for this failure."

Arthur looks into the Irishman's eyes, then down at the floor. Then he turns to the wizard once again. "Yes," he says, "that seems possible." He pauses in thought. "A task, though. What kind of task could we have him do?"

After a silence, Merlin speaks. "He has failed in Ireland, but he has made no enemies that we know of. Could he not return to his homeland and work for you there? Either as emissary, or as spy?"

"Spy?" questions Arthur. "Yes, spy. I need true spies in Ireland, just as I need them among the Picts and the Gauls. Spy. I like that, wizard. I think he might do well as a spy in his own land. What do you say, Irishman?"

Section 69

Niall closes his eyes to think, then opens them. "If I refuse, Leader, do I die?"

Arthur nods.

"Then I have no choice. I will be your spy." He rises and prepares to leave.

"Your first task," Arthur says, "is to bring to me, however you can, Morrigan the witch. Merlin has much to ask her." Merlin laughs, but Niall hears in it a touch of bitterness.

"Morrigan?" Niall asks. He is about to tell Arthur of his encounter with her, but then he decides against it. Instead he smiles, and nods. "Morrigan the witch," he says. "Yes, Leader, that I think I can do." After all, someday surely we will meet in hell, he thinks to himself.

THE END

Turn to section 30.

* 69 *

Another long silence follows. Niall is tired. He has eaten his fill, and the wine has clouded his brain. He drains his cup and Mael fills it again. Niall shakes his head, but his host just smiles. Lifting the silver cup, the Irishman takes one last drink, then lays his head on the table and waits for sleep.

Hands, strong hands, shake him awake. He jerks his head up, then from side to side, in an attempt to clear it. But his vision remains blurred and his hearing distorted. Even the smells—the sweet bread, the oat bread, the clear wine, the fire—have all merged. The room feels hot. Running his tongue over his lips, Niall notices how dry his mouth is. The wine, he thinks to himself, the wine must have done it. He lays his head down once again.

Once more the hands shake him. Now his head begins to pound as the heat and the wine meld within him. Looking up, he sees his host standing above him, and he realizes the hands belong to Mael. The man wants him awake, but Niall does not know why.

The double doors open, and a cool draft from the corridor partly revives him. In walks Brenwin, but now she wears a gown of white with gold trimming the hem and sleeves, and her hair falls in waves over her shoulders and down her back. With her walks Mael the boy, and he is wearing a gray robe that drags on the floor behind him. In his hand he carries a white stick.

Niall shakes his head again, but the vision does not clear. In his eyes Brenwin seems surrounded by a cloud, and the boy's face looks indistinct and old. He holds her hand, and she leads him to the table where he sits beside his grandfather. Struggling to keep his eyes open, Niall feels the wine's assault once again, and his head drops.

This time two pair of hands shake him: the boy's and the old man's. Niall stares hard into the boy's face, and now it is more distinct. Yes, it's him, he thinks. What is he doing here?

The question burns on his lips, but he remembers the fisherman's request and keeps it inside. But then he does not know if silence is the answer, and he opens his mouth as if to speak. Through his blurred vision, he sees Mael the boy and Mael the old man shaking their heads vigorously, holding their fingers to their lips. Niall stares and tries to think with all his draining strength.

If Niall asks about the boy, turn to section 62.

If he holds his silence, turn to section 65.

* 70 *

A shaft of sunlight sears his half-opened eyes, and Niall wakes with a start. Stabbed above the eyes with a sharp pain, he prepares to climb out of bed when he realizes he is lying on a cold stone floor using his pack for a pillow. He sits up, but his head protests vehemently. He lies back down and looks through the rough stone window at a clear blue sky outside.

Puzzled and in pain, his neck and shoulders stiff and his feet sore to the touch, he stands and stretches. He walks to the door to open it, but the old wood rots away and the handle comes off in his hand. Raising his foot, he kicks the panel, and the door breaks in two. Niall steps out into the corridor.

Water drips from above. Looking up, Niall sees large holes in the ceiling and bits of stone fall with the water. Broken stone and rotted wood litter the corridor. Niall walks to the fisherman's dining room, and the double doors fall away at his touch. Inside, a small table supports the remains of an ancient feast, now fuzzy and indistinguishable, the smell overpowering. There is no fireplace in the room.

The witch, Niall thinks. That bloody witch did this

©1986

to me. A spell. I've been under a spell. I must have found this old castle, thought it was the one I was looking for, and gone inside. She provided the rest. Well, that goddamned, evil-minded bitch! If I find her again, I'll tear out her tongue.

Then he groans aloud, "My head hurts, but no wonder there. Sleeping on cold stone. I'll probably die of cold."

He walks to the front door of the castle, and pushes it open, noting its rottenness. As he walks away, Niall looks back on the castle. In the daylight it is decrepit.

The day is long, and the sun shines brightly until, at dusk, it sinks below the horizon in a blaze of crimson and gold. The Irishman keeps the seacoast to his left as he walks towards the north. He has seen nothing strange and met no one all day.

Not until nightfall, when the fresh air and exercise have cleared his head, does Niall realize that he is not on the fisherman's island. He has walked farther than the island is long and, because he has watched the sun, he knows he has not changed direction. I never was there then, he thinks as he lays his head on a pile of soft leaves. The witch again. Part of the spell. He sleeps without dreaming.

In the morning he continues his search, but the coast yields nothing and he begins to head east. He comes to a village, but none there know of the fisherman's castle. At the next village the story is the same. When night falls, Niall enters the woods again, looking for a place to sleep.

He wakes in the night. The moon casts shadows through the trees. An owl calls out.

Suddenly a shadowy figure appears, and Niall leaps

to his feet. The figure approaches. Finding his voice, Niall calls out. "Who are you?" he asks.

"We have met before," says a woman's voice. "I am Morrigan."

Niall's heart pounds. "Bitch!" he calls. "What do you want with me this time?"

"Nothing," the woman replies. She shakes her head. "You are free to go."

Niall's temper flares. "I've always been free to go, you goddamned witch. What makes you think you could keep me here if I wanted to leave?"

"I could make you do more than that, Niall mac Llyr, if I wanted to. But you have won the right to be free." With that, she turns her back and walks away. Niall burns with fury.

If Niall pursues and attacks her, turn to section 63.

If he lets her leave, turn to section 67.

* **71** *

His eyes burning with rage, Niall thrusts his sword at the witch's back. It pierces through the blue-black robe. He draws it forth and sees smeared blood on the point.

The witch stumbles forward, then reaches behind her to touch her back. When she holds her hand to her face, she screams at the sight of her own blood. Reaching into her robe, she draws out a dagger. It gleams silver in the moonlight.

"You have taken your chance, coward!" she cries. "Now it is my turn."

Section 71

At the word "coward" Niall feels something snap inside his brain. With the hoarse yell of a wounded animal, he charges the woman, his sword raised above his head. She jumps away, but again his blade is bloodied. Morrigan backs among the trees, her free hand holding her side.

She stops deep in the woods to support herself against the bulk of an ancient oak. Niall is about to charge once more, when Morrigan straightens and steps away from the tree, only the palm of her hand still flattened against its rough bark. Suddenly he feels a sharp pain inside his head. When it stops, he sees two overlapping Morrigans next to two wavering trees. All the rest is a shapeless blur of forest green and brown.

"What have you done, witch?" he shouts.

Morrigan, whichever one is real, does not reply.

"You're dead, witch!" cries Niall with more bravado than sense. "Your magic cannot help . . ." He is stopped by a searing jolt inside his brain. This time, the pain does not fade quickly and he falls to the ground clutching his head with both hands. His sword, forgotten, falls from his hand to the moldering leaves.

When he can finally raise his head, he sees only a vague black shape staggering towards him. Fighting back the pain, he shakes his head and his vision partly clears. On hands and knees, he gropes about in the leaves and, after what seems like hours of searching, finds his sword. Summoning all his strength, he pulls himself up against a sapling tree and rises to his feet.

The witch is upon him. Her dagger strikes toward his chest. He jerks to the right and feels the dagger sink into his left shoulder. The sharp pain of the wound clears his head. With his right hand he thrusts his sword, and it slides deep between the woman's ribs to pierce her heart. She falls, and his vision clears.

Morrigan lies on the ground, blood running from her mouth. Niall remembers the hag he left behind at the tiny house and waits for the witch to revert to her ugly self. But Morrigan keeps her beauty, and Niall's brow furrows in disbelief.

He walks to her and sees that her eyes are open. She smiles through the blood. "You have your wish, Irishman. I am dying. Are you happy now?"

Niall shakes his head. "Happy . . . no. But I have my revenge, and that's almost as good." He pauses. "You're still beautiful, Morrigan witch. Why?"

"Because this is my real self. The other was my ugly old witch form. I used it often to make the villagers keep their distance, to keep my life to myself. Nothing I do is ugly, warrior. Nothing at all."

Niall spits on the ground. "Don't lie, woman. I went to your bloody castle, and I even grew to love your goddamned little boy. And then it all disappeared. If that isn't ugly, tell me what is." He spits again.

Morrigan smiles, and her eyes roll back in her head.

Turn to section 75.

* **72** *

Cursing both the cold and this new delay, Niall wheels his mount south. He rides in that direction for several miles, then turns to the east once again. Finally, riding without rest, he reaches the sea. From high atop a great white cliff, the sea looks like a mirror, reflecting the moon and the stars on a night filled with the promise of frost.

Niall jumps off his horse, turns it loose, and picks his way down to the shore. There he sleeps, waiting for a ship to come by in the morning. When he awakes, the sky is clear, and he sees a sail up the coast to the north. Making his way there, he hails the ship, swims out to it, and talks his way on board. He arrives in Gaul late that day.

For weeks he wanders, searching for little and finding less. He has no goal, only to avoid meeting Arthur and the Companions, and that he has done by leaving them behind in Britain. He has not accomplished his mission, and to Arthur that means death. But he desires life all the same, and neither Britain nor Ireland offers any place to hide. Not from an avenging king.

One day, on Gaul's western seacoast near Iberia, he spots the remains of a camp in a clearing only fifty yards inside a small forest. Seeing no one, he enters the trees and examines the camp. It has been abandoned in only the last day, he thinks, noticing the fresh smoke smell on the charred wood of the fire. The wood is dry and he is cold, so he sets a fire and warms himself.

If you have marked an "M" on Niall's character record, turn to section 76.

If you have not marked an "M," turn to section 74.

∗ **73** ∗

Niall parries Mael's first thrust, then leaps aside as his countryman follows with a high cut to his right shoulder. Niall whirls and steps in for a slash, but Mael easily turns it aside. Then Mael jabs, and Niall feels a trickle of blood run down the ribs on his left side.

He backs away and readies himself anew. Mael advances, unsmiling. Niall feints high, then cuts toward Mael's legs. Mael slashes downward to parry Niall's cut, but is a second too late. Niall feels his weapon slice through Mael's leggings. Mael jumps away but, when he advances again, Niall notices he is limping.

Niall parries a high lunge, then falls victim to a brilliant low feint followed by a thrust to the neck. Mael's blade opens a gash in the side of his neck, and Niall staggers back. Niall's first blow must have done more damage than can be seen, because his opponent's limp grows worse. Niall awaits his opportunity.

It comes quickly. Mael, now laboring to move, slashes low and then lunges for the kill, but Niall suffers only a shallow cut. As the lunge comes in, Niall steps left, then swings his right fist, weighted by the heavy pommel of his sword, into the side of his opponent's head. Mael falls and, with both hands,

Section 73

Niall raises his sword high in the air by the cross-guard before plunging it into his opponent's heart.

With a quick jerk he releases his sword from the corpse and swings around, just in time to see Starkad the Dane striding toward him, a determined grin on his face. The giant's axe is whirling above his head, gaining momentum for a killing blow. Niall knows that he will not survive a single blow from that axe. His only chance is to evade the berserk Northman.

Niall takes one step backward. The Dane presses on. Niall continues to back up in a circle. He keeps far enough away from Starkad that an axe swing will not land but close enough that a thrown axe will have little momentum. Hardly safe, but as well as he can do.

"Stay still, damn you!" snarls the Dane. Niall locks eyes with him and tries not to glance away at the ever-moving axe. He know the eyes will signal an attack before the hands can move. The circling continues with neither pressing the attack.

Finally Starkad loses patience. Without so much as the blink of an eye, he leaps and swings his axe at Niall's head. Unused to the Dane's style of fighting, Niall reacts late, almost too late. He feels the wind against his face as the axe nearly connects. As the huge blade swings harmlessly by, inches from his face, Niall seizes the advantage he needs. He cuts high, and Starkad parries with the axe. With Starkad's attention focused on their locked weapons, the Irishman kicks hard to the groin. Starkad's eyes widen with pain and, before he can recover, Niall thrusts his sword deep into the giant's abdomen. The Dane falls, and Niall cuts off his hands. The axe clatters away against a rock.

"And now, Irishman," a woman's voice says from behind him, "there is only me." She pauses as Niall turns. "Are you good enough to kill a witch? A Veleda?"

She gestures and Niall's sword drops from his numb fingers. She gestures again and his throat constricts as if powerful hands were crushing his windpipe. One more wave of her hand and the Irishman's knees collapse and he falls heavily to the ground.

But then, as the woman advances toward him, he closes his eyes and centers his concentration within himself. *It is not real!* he chants to himself. *It is not real. It is witchcraft, and I do not believe.* He strains, his muscles tense, and he slowly rises to his knees. His brain hurts, but he repeats to himself, over and over, *I do not believe!* As he opens his eyes, the woman is swaying, her eyes shut tight, and he knows he has won. In an instant the spell leaves him and he rises and strides toward her.

But magic is not her only defense. As fast as lightning, her hand draws forth a knife from her boot. Up it slashes, and Niall feels it pierce his right side. More from reflex than thought, he pulls away and raises his sword high above his head. It comes down with an arm-jolting crack, and the woman's head lies cloven in two.

When his last enemy falls, Niall drops to his knees in exhaustion and relief. He crawls to his foes, makes sure they are truly dead, then rises and stumbles deeper into the woods before falling onto his back. There he sleeps until the sun wakes him at dawn.

Niall mac Llyr wanders the forests and the fields of Gaul for two years, fighting his way across the land in armies and alone until he is known throughout the land for his warfaring talents. "Witchkiller," men call him, and of that name he soon grows proud.

But that name, in the end, proves his nemesis. With the German tribes that swarm into Gaul from the north come witches with spells that kill. These witches do not share, in any way, the love for life and land of the witches of the Celtic tribes. They follow the armies, and on their enemies they practice their necromantic skills in the field of battle. Into one of these battles, riding with the Gallic cavalry, rides Niall, and there he meets his end. For on that field a blackness takes him, and his skin burns with fever, and a flash of fire welds the hilt of his sword to his charred flesh. Pain overtakes him, and he feels himself falling from his horse. The weight of his falling body is borne by his head. He feels the bones in his neck break. Face upward in the bloody dust, he opens his eyes to see the hooves of many horses riding over him. One horse rears high above him, neighing with pain. It falls, and Niall knows no more.

THE END

Turn to section 30.

* **74** *

Out of the woods spring two figures. One is huge and wields an enormous axe. The other, smaller, draws a sword and waits. Mael mac Ronan! he thinks to himself, and Starkad the Dane! The men I managed to avoid in Ireland. A movement among the trees catches his eye, and he sees a third figure, a woman.

"What do you want?" he shouts as he leaps up and draws his sword. "I've done you no harm."

"No, you haven't," says the smaller man. "But you've done us no good, either. For whatever reason, you failed. We can do nothing to change that, but we can make you pay for that failure."

"Failed at what?" Niall shouts again. "You don't even know what I was trying to do."

"*I* do," says the woman, now stepping from between two trees. "I had a message that would have helped you, but you did not choose to receive it."

Niall remembers the conversation he overheard on the road in Ireland, how the two men wanted to deliver a message to him. He had not trusted them then, and he did not now. "How do I know the message would have been useful? All I saw were two men, both of whom looked like they could kill me. I had to stay alive, that was my first goal." He raises his sword.

"Nonetheless, you chose wrong," Veleda replies. "Because of that, much that I love, and all that would have prevented the Saxons from overrunning the ancient glory of my land, will now die. I revere life, Niall mac Llyr, but no longer do I revere yours. I will die, too."

Mael mac Ronan, Irishman and warrior, steps forward. "And because she will die, coward, so will you. How do you care to be killed? Sliced by a sword or chopped by an axe?"

"Neither," says Niall. "I have no intention of dying." With those words he raises his sword, plants his feet, and faces his foes. He looks to the sky and

Section 74

shouts with all the fury and fire of his race, "In the name of Bran my god, I fight prepared to die."

Use the combat rules to determine the winner.

MAEL MAC RONAN
To hit Niall: 14   To be hit: 9   Hit points: 29
Damage with sword: 2 D6+1

STARKAD THE DANE
To hit Niall: 13   To be hit: 10   Hit points: 38
Damage with axe: 2 D6+5

VELEDA
To hit Niall: Make a Constitution roll   To Be Hit: 8
Hit points: 17
Damage with magic: 2 D6 per round

Both men are fighting to the death. If one of them dies, the woman joins the battle, using magic only, beginning the very next round. To determine if she hits with magic, make a Constitution roll each round. If it succeeds, she does not hit that round; if it fails, she does.

If Niall wins, turn to section 73.

If he loses, turn to section 29.

* 75 *

Back through Ireland, then across the water by boat into Britain and toward the eastern coast, Niall journeys. At times he goes on foot; at others, when he can contrive to steal a horse, he rides. But always he sees the ruins of recent battles or hears the rumors of impending ones, and always he must detour either southward or northward. When at last he strikes east without hindrance, he realizes he will pass a scant four or five miles from the camp of Arthur's that he left so long ago. He wants to avoid it, to avoid meeting Arthur again.

On a night in late February, with a cold southeast wind eating through his tunic, he sees torchlights in the distance. Damn! he thinks. A camp! Someone's camp. He does not think it can be Arthur's because it seems too far south, but he cannot be sure. For several minutes he waits in indecision, reining in his anxious mount.

If Niall rides into the camp, turn to section 68.

If he skirts around it, turn to section 72.

* 76 *

"Have you succeeded?" asks a voice in Niall's dream. He opens his eyes to see Mael mac Ronan standing above him. Mael's sword is sheathed at his side, but his hand rests upon the hilt. Niall does not answer, partly from surprise, partly from not wanting to speak. Mael asks the question again. "Have you succeeded, Irishman? Tell me."

Niall bends his head to the ground, then raises it to his countryman's eyes. "No," he says. "It was impossible."

From among the trees strides Starkad the Dane, his axe in his left hand. Behind him walks a woman in a green gown. Niall expects to see the giant, but he stares in wonder at the woman's beauty.

"Veleda," Mael says as a cryptic introduction. "The woman we told you about." And then to Veleda, "He failed. What now?"

"I heard," the woman says. Her voice is calm, but it betrays anxiety and a sense of resignation. "I don't know what now," she continues, and the resignation grows.

Niall stands up and faces the three figures. "I told you it was impossible," he says, "and I believe it was. I didn't succeed in getting Arthur's damned goblet, but I did succeed in almost getting myself killed. I was humiliated and terrified by a witch. I found and lost the love of a child. I failed at the mission, perhaps, but only because there was no way to succeed." He stops and looks straight into the woman's eyes. Into them he stares for nearly a minute, until at last he can hold her angry gaze no longer. "I'm sorry you think I failed. I did my best. Now leave me alone." With that he turns and begins to walk away.

"Come back!" orders Starkad. "We're not finished with you yet."

Niall keeps walking.

Suddenly he hears heavy footfalls behind him. A large hand clasps his shoulder, swinging him around. He looks into the Dane's face. "I said," says the giant, "we aren't done with you yet."

Mael and Veleda walk up behind Starkad. Veleda's eyes pierce Niall's until he cannot tear himself away.

"There was no choice, Irishman," she explains. "None at all. If you didn't succeed fully, you didn't succeed at all. Because the goblet was not found, much that I love—and that you love as well—will disappear. As the dust storm presaged, we will be buried: slowly, perhaps, but completely. We—all of us, all of the ancient race—will disappear under the dust of centuries of distrust, disrespect, and finally disbelief. The Saxons will win. All this time Arthur has won, partly on his own abilities, but mostly because the old ways and the old magic have protected and helped him. Merlin was right, and so was Uther Pendragon. The goblet is essential to the preservation of the Britons, but not for the reasons they believe. The goblet is the center—the magical pulse, I would say—of the ancient ways. It allows life in death. With it gone, we have no chance. From this point on, we have only death in life."

Veleda turns and walks away.

Section 76

"I don't understand!" shouts Niall. "Not half of what you say. What the hell do you mean?" His voice rises with each word.

Starkad the Dane maintains his grip on Niall's shoulder. His fingers dig hard into the Irishman's flesh. "Let me go," Niall snarls. "Let me go NOW!"

Mael says, very calmly, "Let him go, my friend. It won't matter. He has failed my Veleda, and now she will go off and die. The rest doesn't matter." He looks straight at his countryman. "Niall mac Llyr," he says. "Prepare your sword. You have failed Veleda, and you have failed me. Ready yourself to fight to the death."

Use the combat rules to determine the winner. Mael begins the fight with Niall. If Mael is killed, Starkad takes his place, also fighting to the death. If both are killed, Veleda attacks Niall with magic.

MAEL MAC RONAN
To hit Niall: 14   To be hit: 9   Hit points: 29
Damage with sword: 2 D6+1

STARKAD THE DANE
To hit Niall: 13   To be hit: 10   Hit points: 38
Damage with axe: 2 D6+5

VELEDA
To hit Niall: Make a Constitution roll   To be hit: 8
Hit points: 17
Damage with magic: 2 D6+5 per round

If Niall wins, turn to section 73.

If he loses, turn to section 29.

* **77** *

"Old man!" Niall shouts. "The wine. Look at the wine. It's red. It wasn't that color before." When Mael says nothing, Niall asks, more calmly, "Why has the wine turned red?"

Mael the boy looks at Niall and smiles. "It's nothing to worry about, friend Niall. We always serve red wine when the goblets come in. It's got something to do with . . ."

His grandfather interrupts. "I will explain," he says to the boy. "The red wine is necessary, because without it we cannot understand what happens next. Red, as a color, can symbolize much, and only by recognizing the correct symbol can any of this make sense."

Niall remains puzzled, and he shakes his head. "Any of what make sense?" he asks.

"Keep your questions, warrior," the old man says. "You may need them later. For now let me say this: red is vital to our legends and our history. That you should know. The ancients worshipped blood; they sacrificed men for it. Others since have practiced blood sacrifice. For the Romans, of course, red was standard, and for the Britons who defend the island now, red is the color of life. To the Christians, who have by now converted most of the island, red wine stands for the blood of Christ, the possibility of life after death.

"You see, Niall: red is blood, and blood is life. But spilled blood is also death. Life and death: always related, always intertwined."

Section 77

Niall stares at his cup. "I don't know anything about all these symbols, old man, and I'm too damned drunk—or tired—to figure them out now. But even if I did, what does all of this have to do with . . ."

"Stop!" the old man interrupts. Niall looks at him and reads his anxiety. "Don't ask questions unless you have to. That is my request. Remember?"

Niall hesitates, then replies, "Yes. I remember. But you still haven't explained how the wine changed color."

"How do you know it did?" asks the old man. "Maybe it was always that color, and you just couldn't see it." To that Niall does not respond.

Mark a "B" in the Special Events box on Niall's character record. Then read on.

For several minutes Niall remains quiet. The burning desire to question has partly subsided with the discussion about the wine, even though the answers have produced still more questions. He begins to see now that the old man will answer only so many questions, and never more than one or two questions about any one thing. Niall recalls his days of learning in his youth, when his inquisitiveness would finally exasperate his teachers, and they would tell him that nobody was meant to know everything. At the time he thought he was simply too bright for them to handle. Now he wonders if they might have been right. Still, he is frustrated, and still his head pounds. He wishes above all else that his brain and his vision would clear. Everything remains blurred as if in a fog. And now the pressure begins to build again.

If Niall asks about the song, turn to section 78.

If he asks about the goblets, turn to section 81.

If he holds his silence, turn to section 83.

* **78** *

Niall listens, but the words of the song are indistinct. It is the melody he remembers, but even it has no sharpness to it, no definition, only a series of unbased harmonies that waft through the room, embracing all the noises of the night. It is a beautiful song, but it is meaningless. It is without system and without substance.

But still Niall struggles with it. I know it, he thinks to himself. I know it as well as I know my name. Strive as he might, though, nothing comes to him. At last, his head throbbing with the effort of concentration, he turns to Brenwin.

"What is that song, Brenwin? Please. I must know."

Brenwin stops singing. "It is a beautiful song, countryman. One that I have known since I could talk. I am surprised you don't know it."

"I think I do," Niall says. "At least, it haunted me as you sang it, as if it were part of me. Can you sit by me and sing it again?"

"Of course. If that is your wish."

Niall hesitates at Brenwin's statement. Then he nods. "It is," he says. "Right now it's the only thing I wish."

Brenwin sits beside him, and she begins to sing. Her voice haunts, drawing him inside the melody and

Section 78

forcing him inside the words, until at last he sits unmoving, transfixed by the singer and her song.

> Swift chariots
> And horses that carried off the prize
> Once I had many of them.
> I bless the king who sent them.
> My body seeks to make its way
> To the house of judgment.
> When the Son of God knows it is time,
> Let him come to claim his loan.
>
> My arms when they are seen
> Are bony and thin.
> Dear was their practiced craft.
>
> I envy nothing that is old
> Except the Plain of Femhen:
> Even though I wear the thatch of age
> Femhen's crown is yellow still.
> Femhen's crown is yellow still.

There is more, but Niall hears little. The song blends in his mind with the sound of the sea and the crackle of the fire, and the fog returns to the room. Before Brenwin has finished, Niall is asleep.

Turn to section 70.

* **79** *

Starkad leads Niall toward a camp not far from his own. Here stand two small tents with a small fire between them. From one of them emerge a man and a woman, both dressed warmly and both smiling. Niall recognizes the man as Mael mac Ronan, but he does not know the woman.

"I am Veleda," she says. "Welcome."

"You are beautiful," replies Niall, more as a realized thought than a response to her words. The men laugh.

"You have brought the goblet," is her only response, and her smile is wide. "How can I thank you?"

Niall thinks for a moment, then states his only need. "I am cold, and I need some food. If you give me that, I won't ask anything else."

"Easily granted," Veleda says, and she turns and enters her tent. When she returns, she spreads a blanket before the fire, and sets on it food that, even though it is simple, Niall considers a feast. Only after he has eaten does she speak again.

"May I see it?"

Niall opens his sack and gives her the red cloth in which the goblet is wrapped. She removes the wrapping and holds the treasure aloft. Then, speaking a few soft words, she brings it to her lips and kisses it. Without cleaning it or emptying it of its dust, she returns it to its wrap.

"Do you know that I must keep it?" she asks.

Section 79

Niall nods. "Yes," he says. "I've known that all along. It's yours. I won't try to take it from you."

"Good," Veleda replies. She smiles at him. "You did the right thing to bring it to me, and now you do another by letting me keep it. You are wise, Niall mac Llyr."

"No," responds the Irishman without hesitation. "I am no more wise now than I was before Merlin sent me out. But I have learned enough to know that some things are not meant to be mine, even though I might find them and hold them for a while. Something brought this thing to you, and that same thing now tells me you are meant to keep it. That takes no wisdom, my lady. I didn't figure it out myself."

Veleda smiles again, and looks at Mael. "He is indeed wise, Mael, and I think we might keep him with us, if he would stay."

Starkad the Dane stares at her in disbelief. "Him?" he almost shouts. "What can *he* do for us?"

But it is Mael, and not Veleda, who answers him. "Among other things, my friend, he can keep you in check and stop you from running all over the countryside during the night, terrorizing every Gaul you can find. But Veleda is right. He has proven a certain kind of worth, and I think we can use that." Then, looking at Niall, he asks, "Would you join us, countryman?"

Niall looks at the three, then down at the ground. Finally he lifts his head and says, "Yes. I will join you." And then to their smiles he says. "But only on one condition."

"And what's that?" asks Mael.

"Just this," Niall says. "I'd like Veleda to tell me what the goblet is supposed to do."

Mael looks at the woman, who nods. "Nothing," she says.

"What do you mean, nothing?"

"That's the point of this whole thing. The right goblet means that nothing changes. Arthur will go on as he is destined, as will you, and Starkad, and Mael, and everyone else. Nothing will change. That's why it was filled with dust. It simply *was,* and things that simply *are* let the earth form around them. It was the only goblet that would allow that."

"You mean," asks Niall, perplexed, "that I did all this for nothing?"

"So that nothing would be changed from its present course, yes," replies Veleda. "That is why you had to bring it to me. Merlin wanted to change Arthur's destiny; his goblet would have made that possible. But no matter how good something like that might seem at first, it always ends in evil. Only one destiny is right. When you chose the correct goblet, you ensured that all would continue. The choice was exactly right."

Niall stares at her, unbelieving. Then he rises, looks at them all, and offers Starkad his sword. The Dane hesitates, but then takes it and lays it on the ground. Then he grasps Niall's hand and smiles an awkward smile, and the four companions begin the remainder of their yet unfinished story.

THE END

Turn to section 30.

* **80** *

"No," replies Niall. "I have no reason to come with you."

"You don't understand, Irishman," the Dane says. "If you do not come willingly, I will bring you whatever way I can. Veleda wants to see you."

"Why?"

"She will tell you." The giant pauses. "Now, will you come willingly, or will I have to carry you to her? Decide!"

If Niall goes willingly, turn to section 79.

If he still refuses, turn to section 85.

* **81** *

"There are three goblets," Niall says. "Why? I was waiting for one, not three."

At the sound of Niall's question, the old man stands up. Reaching for his cane, he struggles around to Niall's side of the table and seats himself in the chair beside him. The boy, too, has stopped what he is doing and watches the two men intently. Only Brenwin seems unaffected. Her role in this, it appears, is already set, and she performs it to perfection. Taking each goblet in turn, she lifts them toward Niall and sets them down in front of him. Then she turns and, grasping the golden tray, promptly leaves the room.

The three goblets form a line. The bright gold one is on Niall's left, the dust-covered one in the center, and the dust-filled one on the right. Each exudes a warm red glow, subdued in proportion to the amount of dust covering that glow. Niall stares at all three of the goblets, then lifts his hand toward the first.

The old man's hand clamps his wrist. Niall struggles briefly but then surrenders, astonished at Mael's strength. By this time, the boy has seated himself on Niall's right side, and he too seems ready to stop Niall's reach. The Irishman does not bother to test young Mael's power.

The old man speaks. "Don't touch them, my friend. Not yet."

Niall looks at him. "Why not? What difference does it make? How will I know which is the right goblet?"

"That's just the point," continues the fisherman. "You don't know which is the right goblet, and neither do I. Nor the boy. I have long known the choice would have to be made, but none have ever come this far. You are the first to ask, perhaps the first to see. I didn't know the choice would be this difficult."

He points toward the goblets. "Look at them, Niall. Look at their differences. Look at how each is calculated to be a possible choice. The one on the left gleams, its designs glowing in the light from the fire. The image is of an oak, a mighty oak sprawling towards the sun. A sign of the Druids, Niall, the mighty ones whom many think can yet save us from both the Saxons and the Britons. If you choose this goblet, will you not be a savior among your own people?"

Niall stares at it, and into his mind comes a vision of peace, of antiquity come to life. Gods and heroes, Bran and Brigit and Finn and Cu Chulainn, all of them with arms outstretched, as if calling them to him. He sees the gleam of the sun on the sea, and white sails billowing on their way to war, and majestic burial stones standing tall on the plain, glowing with a golden light. But when he looks away, his mind clouds once again, and the vision is gone.

"Or this one," the old man continues, pointing to the center goblet. "It too is gold, but dust covers whatever engravings its sides might contain. Perhaps it has none; perhaps they are subtle and beautiful. Doesn't its very mystery almost force you to choose it?"

Niall's mind races back to Merlin's explanation, of dust covering the red jewel, of dust about to cover all life. Life and death merge all about him here, he thinks. Everything about this place provides a link between those two great powers. And this, surely, is Merlin's goblet. A thin layer of dust obscures the red glow, and no ornaments appear on the side. Niall longs to take it from the table, to wipe it clean and polish it till it outgleams even the first goblet, and then to run with it far from the fisherman's castle, back to the waiting king.

Slowly his hand inches toward it. This time both Maels clamp down on the hand before it goes very far.

"And this one, Niall," the old fisherman continues, pointing toward the third goblet. "What is the meaning of the dust that fills it to its top? Do you not long to know? It is gold, that is plain, and we see that it bears designs, but again a coating of dust blocks our view. It too glows red, but this red pales beside the other two, which shine brighter and stronger. Can you tell, warrior, what *this* goblet might mean?"

At this goblet, too, Niall stares, and before his eyes the room darkens. The fire seems to die almost to a spark, and the warm red light inside the goblets dies with it. The old man's skin now seems to flap loosely on his face, and wrinkles deepen visibly. The young boy grown suddenly old, his hand, still gripping Niall's wrist, now bony and marked heavily with jutting veins. The table smells of rot, and the stone walls drip filth. Niall feels overcome by a sudden urge to sleep, the weight of his clothes too much for him to bear. His eyes begin to close, this time, he hopes, they will finally let him sleep.

But the old man's voice pierces his mind, and the vision of old age and of death is gone. "The time has come," old Mael says, "the time I have awaited for many long years. The time has come, Niall mac Llyr, for one of the goblets to be chosen. You need not choose quickly, but if you wait until dawn the chance will no longer be there. You have two hours. The boy and I will leave. When you decide, merely touch your chosen goblet. Do not touch any of them beforehand. Now, my friend, my blessing."

The young boy and the old man rise from their seats. Taking his grandfather's hand, the boy leads the way through the double doors. The doors slam, and Niall is alone.

Once again he examines the goblets. Nothing has changed. The first still gleams, the second rests under its dusty film, and the third remains filled with dust. Niall looks aside and stares for a moment at the fire. It cracks and bursts and jumps like before, but something seems to have gone out of it. He rises from the table to inspect the fire and realizes that it has grown weaker. Puzzled, he walks back to his seat before the goblets.

I'm not going to hurry, he tells himself. I have to think. The dawn, Mael has said, is but two hours off, but two hours is ample time to make a choice. He vows to sit at the table, ignore the time, and wait until his choice is certain.

Niall stares at the three goblets, but from them he learns nothing. Time passes. The Irishman glances at the fire, and he sees that it is even lower than before. It's counting the time! Niall thinks with surprise. The fire is my hourglass.

"It can't be," he murmurs. If it's an hourglass, it's dying too fast, he says to himself. I haven't spent half my time, but the fire is less than half as strong. But if it isn't measuring the time, what *is* it measuring?

An image comes to him of Mael the fisherman, and in that vision the old man lies motionless upon his bed. The boy kneels beside him, his hands joined in prayer, and Brenwin places a cloth on the fisherman's forehead. The fisherman is dying, and now Niall knows the fire is dying with its maker. It will not be two hours before it goes out. I have less than two hours, Niall thinks. Much less, to judge by the fire. Why didn't he tell me that?

But no answer comes. Niall continues to stare, now at the fire, now at the goblets, yet he comes no closer to the choice he knows he must make.

Perhaps the pressure of time sharpens Niall's mind, because he suddenly understands the goblets in a different way. As if something has forced him to open his thoughts, he realizes that he has considered the goblets and what they stand for in only one fashion. In the first goblet he saw only the glory of the past, and the possibility of its return. The second goblet was the most attractive, because it was the goblet that Merlin wanted, and the one Niall knew most about. In the third, he saw only blackness and death.

Now he sees them anew. The first, with its golden gleam and towering oak, still reflects the beauty of the past, but now it shows as well the extreme danger of dreaming of that past. To relive the past, Niall suddenly sees, is to destroy the present and perhaps even the future. It occurs to him also that the past *has* no future; past is past, and cannot advance. Yet the images are so strong—the golden sunset; the great, green land; the power of the oak, and the sheer joy of ancientness—that the dangers seem almost unreal.

The second goblet, too, now shows a different side. For Niall it still holds the greatest attraction, because it is the one he knows best, the one whose explanation means the most to him. But now he begins to question both the explanation and the motives of the person who gave it to him. The dust covers all, including the red glow, which according to Merlin symbolizes life. But what if the red is a symbol of death instead? Wouldn't the dust then be a good thing, a valiant attempt to bury evil? In that case, to remove the dust would be to remove the only good that exists. Niall's head spins with the meaning of his thoughts and the heat of the room, hot even though the fire has almost died.

To Niall, though, the third goblet presents the

greatest enigma. Filled with dust, it barely allows the red glow to shine forth. At first the goblet suggested death and blackness, burial and obscurity, and his mind had been pulled into that dark hole. But now it strikes the Irishman, strangely enough, as perhaps more life-filled than either of the other goblets. Two ideas come to him. First: if the glow of the red jewel shines through, even though the goblet is filled with dust, doesn't that suggest that good is buried and need only be dug up? Second: if the red jewel is so powerful that it can make itself known even though the entire earth attempts to conceal it, isn't it better that it remain concealed? Perhaps the jewel itself is evil, and perhaps the dust is needed to keep it under control. Perhaps the jewel is—and at this Niall shakes his head—the very ruler of death itself. In that case, it is the best choice of the three goblets.

But none of these ideas is fully formed, and none is very helpful. All Niall decides is that symbols are useless. He can interpret them in any way he wants, and each interpretation is true for that moment, but in the end he must choose one of the three goblets, and no amount of reasoning can help him make the choice. Maybe it doesn't matter which one he picks; maybe any of the three will do as well. Maybe, in fact, none of them will do anything. He also knows that he can't take that chance. Something—beyond his ability to comprehend—is taking place here, something that can decide his own future and maybe even the future of his world. He is tempted now, because he can think no more, to simply close his eyes and reach out with his hand. But that, too, is impossible, because then he would never know, and the possibility of knowing is now all that keeps him in the game.

If Niall selects the first goblet, gleaming gold with oak designs, turn to section 82.

If he chooses the second goblet, the one with the thin film of dust, turn to section 84.

If he chooses the third, the goblet filled with dust, turn to section 86.

If he walks away and chooses none of them, turn to section 70.

* **82** *

Niall walks through fields of tall grass, the golden light of sunset glowing behind him. He is peaceful; memories of the fisherman, and Uther Pendragon, and the gleaming gold goblet, fade swiftly from his mind. There is no reason for him to remember. He is in Ireland, and the country of his birth casts its eyes to its future on the foundations of its past. A giant oak sways gently above him, the birds perched in its branches calling sharply across the coming night. It is beautiful, Niall thinks. Beautiful beyond words.

Three more weeks he walks, and in that time his memory of the quest dies completely. Through villages crowded with chanting merchants, singing bards, laughing children, the Irishman now passes, where the priests practice prophecy and the dead are buried beneath the standing stones, from whence they wend their way down to Annwn, the unknown land of the dead. Day by day the sun is gold, until the rainclouds form black in the sky and release their gentle rains down upon the grass.

Section 83

Niall's wanderings take him to an eastern port, and there he finds a place to stay and a woman to love. As the Irish sun rises golden on the morning of the feast of Samhain, Niall mac Llyr looks out on the rolling green hills that make their way to the sea. He smiles on the day and turns his back, forever, upon his unremembered past.

THE END

Turn to section 30.

* **83** *

Slowly, holding his cup in both hands, Niall lifts the wine to his mouth. It is warm, and it does not flow, but slithers, down his throat. Gagging, Niall drops the cup, and the wine, now thick and clinging, oozes from it onto the table. The startled Irishman jumps back from the table, points to the red stream, and screams, "What is it?!" And then he falls to his knees and vomits from the depths of his stomach. Exhausted and drained, he closes his eyes for a moment, but sleep overtakes him.

Turn to section 70.

* **84** *

As he approaches the camp of Arthur the king, Niall begins to feel the harsh, dry dust eating at his eyes and throat. Every breath burns him, and he feels the grit settle into the wrinkles of his skin. Opening his flagon, he takes a long drink, then covers it and rides on.

A sentry greets him. "Who approaches?" demands the tall, burly man, and Niall does not recognize him as one of the Companions. "Who are you and what do you want?" the sentry repeats when Niall does not answer.

"I am Niall mac Llyr," he replies at last, "and I am here to see the king. I have something for him."

"I'll bet you do," intones the guard. "Lately, many people bring gifts to Arthur."

Niall does not need this; the dust is annoyance enough. "Just tell your king," he commands, "that Niall mac Llyr has his precious goblet. If you don't, I will kill you. Now move!"

The guard stand startled for a moment, then turns and walks quickly toward the center of the camp. A few minutes later, he returns with a message for Niall to dismount and follow him. He leads the Irishman directly into Arthur's tent.

"Welcome, Irishman," the Leader of the Britons says. "I hear congratulations are due. You have accomplished your mission."

"I have," says Niall. Then, handing him a small leather sack, he says, "Now may I go? This dust is horrible."

"Wait," replies Arthur. "There is more I'd like to know. And you might as well stay to see if your accomplishment is worth anything." The king laughs. Niall does not.

The king hands the sack to Merlin the wizard, who opens it and takes out a red cloth bundle. Unwrapping the bundle, he smiles broadly and holds up the goblet. Niall has done nothing to it, neither cleaned it nor polished it. Nor, in fact, has he even looked at it since he took it from the fisherman's table. As soon as he had made his choice, Mael the boy entered the room and screamed through tears, "He's dead, Niall. He's dead." And then the boy collapsed.

Niall ran to him, but Brenwin reached him first. A look of hatred in her eyes kept Niall back. As she stepped between him and the boy, a clear gesture of protection, Niall realized what he had done. He had made either a huge mistake or a huge sacrifice. Either way, he didn't like it.

Now he stands in Arthur's tent, only half-interested in the answer. He stares at the wizard, who now polishes the dust from the goblet, and suddenly feels that his choice must have been wrong. He hates Merlin, and when he looks over at Arthur he finds that he hates him at least as much. He has gone in search of an elusive artifact, and he has succeeded, but in the process he learned what it means to lose something very precious. Maybe the choice of goblet was right. The journey, he is now sure, was wrong.

"May I go?" he asks again.

"Yes," says Arthur. "But I don't understand your hurry."

Niall shrugs. "Have you never fought so hard for

something, Leader, only to realize in the end that you don't care? Has someone ever taken something from you that you didn't want to lose?" He pauses. "Have you ever lost a victory?"

The king of the Britons looks puzzled. "No. Never. You speak like an Irishman, Niall mac Llyr, in riddles. And riddles are something I don't like. You may leave."

Niall walks to the exit, then turns around. He shakes his head. "I didn't think so," he says, then wheels and strides away.

Niall mac Llyr walks to the edge of the camp, then climbs onto his horse and gallops swiftly away. At his back, although he does not see it, the dust slowly rises into the sky, leaving Arthur's camp clear and clean. He does not see Arthur emerge from his tent and command his Companions to go into the land and spread the news that Arthur has found Joseph's lost goblet. He does not hear Arthur tell Merlin to journey into the last, remaining Druid strongholds, to tell them of Arawn, Lord of the Underworld's, famous cup and the benefits they might receive from it.

In the months to come, Niall hears reports of Arthur's victories, as the British king forces the Saxons farther and farther from the interior, back in disarray toward the coast. He hears as well the worship of the people all over Britain, who now proclaim their king as hero and deity. And he hears, if only in his sleep, the roar of the man-bear of Uther Pendragon as the dead king rises and fights his monstrous foe and wins the freedom of final death. But the Irishman rides a gray ship to the continent, where he wanders lost in thought until he dies. Of Arthur's glory and of the grand future of the British people, he simply does not care.

THE END

Turn to section 30.

* 85 *

His axe in his right hand, Starkad the Dane advances. Niall waits, his sword drawn and his shield ready. Finally there is only a foot of ground between them, and the two combatants know that one of them is about to die.

Use the combat rules to determine the winner.

STARKAD THE DANE
To hit Niall: 13   To be hit: 10   Hit points: 38
Damage with axe: 2 D6+5

If Niall wins, turn to section 87.

If he loses, turn to section 29.

* **86** *

The forest is cold at night, and Niall looks up through the trees into the sky at black clouds laden with snow. He shivers, then shifts in his blanket, but still the frost eats its way under his skin. Finally, despite his exhaustion, he gives up on sleep and looks for kindling. He needs a fire.

Fire. His mind goes back to the roaring flame in the dining chamber of the fisherman's castle. There he was hot and his mind was dull, where now he is cold and his mind is as crisp as the night. In his mind, Niall sees again Mael the boy, racing through the double door and into Niall's arms, and Brenwin running, her white gown flowing behind her, to embrace them both. He hears again the sound of sea, its laughing waves now dancing along the coast as it overcomes at last the creatures that sought to destroy its song. Again he remembers the fire, its blaze now restored, burning hot and bright and leaping along the walls. Into the room walks Mael the fisherman, tall and proud, his cane now held aloft in a gesture of victory and of thanks.

To Niall, who now shivers in the forests of northern Gaul, the memory is warm. He remembers leaving the castle long before Brenwin and the two Maels had finished their celebration, sneaking out at dawn with the dust-filled goblet gripped firmly in his hand. He had needed no guide, for his mind began to clear as he continued to the east. At last, after six long weeks of boats and horses and tough miles on foot, he had arrived in Gaul. Now his head was completely

Section 86

clear, and the goblet had ceased being a guide. This forest, he knows, is where he must be.

With the fire now lit, the Irishman wanders a short distance in search of food. Berries he finds by the handful, and other plants—good for their roots—he gathers in his arms, but only after an hour of searching does he spot a rabbit. Putting the other food on the ground, he quietly draws his sword, then stalks the animal until he is only a few feet behind it. One slash, and the rabbit's head falls to the ground. Niall's stomach growls at the very thought of the meal to come.

But when he returns, the fire is out. Standing above it is an enormous figure, hidden in the shadows of the trees. Crouching, Niall drops everything but the sword, then stands up and commands, "Who are you?" The figure steps out from among the shadows.

"Starkad the Dane!" Niall exclaims.

"Yes," comes the reply. "Starkad. I have come to find you, Irishman. Veleda wants to see you. Will you come with me willingly?"

If Niall agrees to accompany Starkad, turn to section 79.

If he refuses, turn to section 80.

* **87** *

Niall takes one step backward. The Dane presses on. Niall continues to back up in a circle. He keeps far enough away from Starkad that an axe swing will not land but close enough that a thrown axe will have little momentum. Hardly safe, but as well as he can do.

"Stay still, damn you!" snarls the Dane. Niall locks eyes with him and tries not to glance away at the ever-moving axe. He knows the eyes will signal an attack before the hands can move. The circling continues with neither man pressing the attack.

Finally Starkad loses patience. Without so much as the blink of an eye, he leaps and swings his axe at Niall's head. Unused to the Dane's style of fighting, Niall reacts late, almost too late. He feels the wind against his face as the axe nearly connects. As the huge blade swings harmlessly by, inches from his face, Niall seizes the advantage he needs. He cuts high, and Starkad parries with the axe. With Starkad's attention focused on their locked weapons, the Irishman kicks hard to the groin. Starkad's eyes widen with pain and, before he can recover, Niall thrusts his sword deep into the giant's abdomen. The Dane falls, and Niall cuts off his hands. The axe clatters away against a rock.

With an ungodly scream, into the fight jumps Mael mac Ronan, waving his sword high above his head. The sight of his fallen comrade seems to madden him, and as he prepares to strike he screams a battle cry of fury and of hatred.

Section 88

Use the combat rules to determine the winner.

MAEL MAC RONAN
To hit Niall: 14   To be hit: 9   Hit points: 29
Damage with sword: 2 D6+1

If Niall wins, turn to section 88.

If he loses, turn to section 29.

* **88** *

Niall parries Mael's first thrust, then leaps aside as his countryman follows with a high cut to his right shoulder. Niall whirls and steps in for a slash, but Mael easily turns it aside. Then Mael jabs, and Niall feels a trickle of blood run down the ribs on his left side.

He backs away and readies himself anew. Mael advances, unsmiling. Niall feints high, then cuts toward Mael's legs. Mael slashes downward to parry Niall's cut, but is a second too late. Niall feels his weapon slice through Mael's leggings. Mael jumps away but, when he advances again, Niall notices he is limping.

Niall parries a high lunge, then falls victim to a brilliant low feint followed by a thrust to the neck. Mael's blade opens a gash in the side of his neck, and Niall staggers back. Niall's first blow must have done more damage than can be seen, because his opponent's limp grows worse. Niall awaits his opportunity.

It comes quickly. Mael, now laboring to move, slashes low and then lunges for the kill, but Niall suffers only a shallow cut. As the lunge comes in, Niall steps left, then swings his right fist, weighted by the heavy pommel of his sword, into the side of his opponent's head. Mael falls and, with both hands, Niall raises his sword high in the air by the crossguard before plunging it into his opponent's heart.

For the remainder of his days, Niall wanders through Gaul, fighting to survive and searching for the answer to his goblet. Once every night, he removes the goblet from his sack and unwraps it from its protective cloth, but it never shows him where it must go. One night he sees a woman, tall and beautiful, searching for something in the forest, and remembering both sympathy and desire he almost goes to her. But then he remembers his treasure, and he fears for its safety. When she leaves, he disappears deeper into the trees.

He sees her again, almost two months later. She is singing, now, a song about death and the end of all things. From her lips comes the name Mael mac Ronan, and the words of the song speak of a giant axeman who died for nothing. Again Niall almost stirs from his hiding place. But once more concern for the goblet overpowers him, and he waits till she leaves before running far away.

Finally, in the snow-filled forests of the north, past even the great Germanic sea, he meets his end. Weak with hunger and sick with fever, the Irishman struggles with each step to hide his precious goblet from the sight of all men. His frost-covered eyes do not see the white wolves silent in the snow, and his frozen skin does not feel their teeth sink deeply into him. For a short moment, a running red covers the white of the ground, but within seconds the wind hides all

signs of the struggle. Only an old cup, tarnished and bent, remains of the half-eaten man.

THE END

Turn to section 30.

Turn to section 30.

* **89** *

Astonished, Lightbeard drops the cup he has been drinking from. With the smaller man out of the way, Niall faces the fair-haired, knife-wielding bandit.

"Who are you?" growls Lightbeard.

"You won't know me," Niall replies. "So why bother asking?"

"What do you want?"

"Your sword, and your shield, and your rabbit. Will you give them to me?"

Lightbeard laughs, but the sound is neither friendly nor generous.

"Then fight for them," Niall yells, and charges his foe.

The bearded man fights well, but Niall has the edge of experience. He was a skilled fighter before he met the Companions, and several days of watching and training with them has honed his skill considerably.

He dances away from Lightbeard's knife thrusts, waiting for the one opening he needs to make this fight short. The only way he can lose, he knows, is to strike too soon, to give the advantage to his opponent.

Lightbeard grows frustrated. Slash after slash of his knife miss the quick-reflexed Irishman. Cunningly he slows his movements, but Niall knows it is merely a trick. He is ready when Lightbeard makes his move.

Both men are breathing shallowly and taking a moment to rest when Lightbeard suddenly attacks. He leaps at Niall, his knife aimed for the throat. It is the move Niall has been waiting for. He steps to his left, extending his right arm and the sword into his opponent's path. A second later, Lightbeard has impaled himself on it.

"You were quick," Niall says to the corpse, "but not quick enough."

As he stoops to wipe his sword on the bandit's tunic, Niall hears a noise behind him. Rising and turning in one motion, he sees the smaller man charging toward him. Niall ducks just in time, but the knife gashes his arm. It hurts like hell, but he has no time to be concerned about the pain.

Darkbeard turns and charges again. *What an ass!* Niall thinks. *How often does he think he can get away with this? Well, what's good for one is good for the other.* The Irishman aims his sword in his foe's path and waits for the easy victory.

But Darkbeard surprises him. Ten feet from the Irishman he stops, aims his knife, and throws it. Niall, braced to receive the running body on his sword, raises his weapon only by reflex, but in his surprise he is too late. The knife buries itself deep into his stomach, and the Irishman drops his sword and collapses. The bearded man picks up Lightbeard's knife, walks to his foe, and drives it into Niall's heart.

Turn to section 29.

* **90** *

Niall moves first. He aims a quick slash at Redbeard's legs. Redbeard parries it, then jumps back. The two men circle, both watchful for a mistake. Suddenly Redbeard opens up the fight. With a yell, he charges.

Surprised but prepared, Niall ducks his opponent's high swing, then whirls and thrusts at Redbeard's back as he runs by. He draws blood, but not enough. Redbeard grunts, then turns and walks back to the fight. Over Redbeard's shoulder, Niall sees Blackbeard rising to his feet. *I must strike now,* he thinks. *Two may be too much.*

A leap into the middle, a parry of Redbeard's slash, a feint to the legs, and a cut to the head. More blood, and Redbeard staggers, but he is not out yet. Lunging away from the bandit's next thrust, Niall sees Blackbeard's knife flying toward his eyes and instinctively he ducks. The sudden movement puts him off balance and, before he can recover, he feels cold steel slicing through his neck.

Turn to section 29.

* **91** *

The horse rears, high above the frightened Irishman. Niall jumps back, his reflexes making up for his astonishment. He examines his weapon but, majestic as it is, it has nothing on Uther's legendary sword,

Caliburn. One thrust from Caliburn, Niall knows, and it will all be over.

Down swings Caliburn, and Niall leaps for his life. He picks himself up off the ground but stumbles backward into a boulder. Leaping atop it, he braces himself and awaits Uther's charge. Running from the specter, he knows, is useless.

The charge comes quickly, and with it comes the battle cry of a soul in torment. So ghastly is it, so haunting, that Niall is frozen, his mind cleared of thought and his body shuddering. Down on the paralyzed Irishman sweeps the ghost of Uther Pendragon, and Niall barely manages to raise his shield in his terror. Caliburn sweeps down cleaving the shield in two.

The fight is over. Niall stands defenseless on the rock, unable to watch as the killing blow descends.

Turn to section 29.

* **92** *

As the huge beast lumbers toward him, Niall draws his sword and turns to face it. He knows it is strong, and he must stay out of its reach. Backing away from it, he extends the sword as far as he can in front of him, hoping the beast will grab for it. If it does, he can thrust hard into its chest.

Seeing the sword, the man-bear slows. Then it snarls, and the snarl chills Niall's blood. But he does not waver. He backs up one step, then another, then still another, as he holds the bear at bay.

But suddenly he runs out of room. The stone slab presses into his back. He slides slowly along it to his right, then stops and waits. *Hold*, he tells himself. *Wait for just the right* . . .

With wicked, yellow claws extended, the man-bear's arm swings toward him, its speed wholly unexpected. The Irishman ducks, but the force of the blow throws him across the room. Before he can move, the man-bear is on him. Niall slashes at its legs, and the sword bites through, but it is too late. The beast strikes again, and again, and with one final blow it smashes Niall's skull.

Turn to section 29.

* **93** *

The man-bear lies dead on the stone floor. Its body shows the slashes from Niall's sword, and its tongue dangles from its head. But the man-bear does not bleed. Cautiously, Niall crouches down and touches it; it is ice cold. Certain then that the beast will not move, Niall thrusts his left hand into one of the wounds. Inside, too, it is cold, and his hand emerges unbloodied.

Suddenly the man-bear shudders. Niall jumps to his feet and readies his sword. The beast rolls onto its side and begins to sit up. Tensed, Niall steps towards it. He raises his sword, about to swing, when a cold voice from behind stops him.

"Leave him," it commands. Then, more sadly, "Leave him in peace. He can no longer hurt you."

Niall turns and looks behind. The body is sitting on the stone slab, and it now looks to Niall more like a living body than a skeleton. Its eyes stare at the beast that now struggles its way back to the spot where

Niall first saw it. Once there, it sits again, but its hands now rest on the floor at its sides.

"Get me my robe," the voice commands. Niall barely questions his obedience, so authoritative is the sound of that cold voice. He reaches for the purple robe and rests it on the body's shoulders. The body lifts itself off the slab and stands upright. Then it looks at the awe-struck Irishman.

"Can you talk, warrior?" it asks. "You have said nothing all the while you have been here."

"I can," Niall replies. His voice sounds out of place here, a living voice in a chamber of death.

"Then tell me who you are and what you are doing here."

For a brief moment Niall fights his impulse to tell all to this uncanny stranger. The body's gaze is hard and demanding, and what it demands seems to Niall suddenly all too reasonable. Slowly at first, but with growing enthusiasm and even excitement, he tells of the dust storm and of the goblet, of Merlin's visit and of the journey across the Salisbury plain. He talks long, but the body does not interrupt.

"Merlin sent you, then?" asks the body when Niall has finished. Niall nods. "So Merlin is still alive," the body muses. "That is good. For Arthur, at least."

A long pause follows. Then the body continues. "Merlin would have you find the specter of Uther Pendragon and get advice from him . . . advice about a mysterious goblet that Arthur wants. And where do you think this specter is?"

"I don't know," says Niall. "I'm exhausted, and all I want is to sleep. And eat, if there was anything here." His eyes close involuntarily.

"Yes, of course," says the body. "I had forgotten.

Forgotten much. But now I am reminded, and the memory is not sweet. I always thought it would be." It looks at Niall, who shakes his head in an attempt to stay awake. "Go to sleep, Niall mac Llyr. You will awaken in the crypt of Uther Pendragon whom you seek, but unlike him, you will still be alive. Go to sleep, and I will find food." The body walks through the entrance and disappears down the passageway.

"Pendragon," mumbles Niall. "I've found him, then." He sprawls on the stone slab, and falls into a deep sleep.

He wakes to the smell of roasting meat. Sitting up, he surveys the stone chamber around him. The man-bear sits motionless in the middle of the floor, the red robe once again covering him. Near the entrance, a small fire roasts a fat rabbit, and near the fire is a pail of water. The body is gone.

Niall drinks some of the water in the pail, then splashes some on his face. He devours the rabbit and drinks again. As he is finishing, he looks up and sees in the entranceway the purple-robed figure that left him hours ago. Uther Pendragon has grown younger and seems now a fit age to be the father of Arthur. Niall swallows and says, "I thank you. The rabbit was excellent."

Uther nods. "I'm glad you enjoyed it. What little skill I had in cookery has been long out of use. If you are finished with your meal, we must talk. I have little time, as Merlin well knew." He walks to the stone slab and sits on it.

"I was Uther Pendragon. I am no longer alive, even though your senses deny that. But while I was alive, I knew of Arthur's precious goblet and, like Arthur, I wanted it badly. With its strange power, I thought, I could at last end the strife between Druid and Christian, and have both fight against the enemies that do not stop coming.

"The goblet, or so the legend goes, was brought to this island by a man named Joseph. Why he brought it here no one knows. Where he put it no one knows, either, although I think I have some idea. I died, I am sure, because of that knowledge."

Niall sits up. "But what is the goblet?" he asks.

"Forgive my impatience," says the body. "I forgot to explain. What the goblet is depends upon whom you listen to. According to the Christians, the goblet is the cup that Christ drank from during his last meal with his followers. If that is true, then it has great power: the power to transform and to nourish, perhaps without limit. It also grants strength and belief. If you listen to the Druids, though, the goblet has similar powers, but it is the property of hell itself. It judges those who die by preventing cowards from drinking from it.

"To be honest, Irishman, I cared little for its religious significance. I wanted it because it would give me the power to unite my people. Both Druid and Christian would willingly follow—maybe even worship—any ruler who possessed Joseph's goblet. Its power was to give me power, and I sought for it long and hard, but in the end I failed. But I learned something important, Niall mac Llyr. I learned that the goblet has a price. It is cursed."

"Cursed?" Niall almost shouts. "I don't deal with things that are cursed. I hate them."

"Then you will not be dealing with Joseph's goblet, either," the body says calmly. "And if that is the case, you have no business here." He lowers himself onto the slab.

"No, wait," Niall says, starting towards the slab. "I see that I must deal with it, or else I'll fail completely. It's just that 'cursed' is not a word I even like to think about. That's all."

The body of Uther Pendragon sits up again. "And who of us does, warrior? Do you think my memories of being cursed are any more pleasant than my other memories? In early life I did not believe in curses; later I believed they existed, but not that they could affect me. Before I died, I finally believed both. But by then it was too late."

As if enchanted by the body's icy voice, Niall says nothing. After two long, silent minutes, the voice continues. "You fear curses, Irishman. But a curse need not harm you, not if you know what to do about it. I did not, and many besides me have not known either. All of us have died or lived out miserable lives under the curse's power. The curse against me was of the first kind. It killed me.

"The goblet itself is not cursed. It could never be cursed, because it is beyond the powers of curse whether you believe in its Druidic or its Christian origins. But knowing something about the goblet— where it lies, what it does, how it arrived—curses the knower, perhaps automatically, perhaps not. This curse is so powerful that the knowledge need not be definite; any idea might be enough to trigger the curse. In my case, I knew only two things. One was that the goblet, as I have told you, is a provider of some sort. The other is the goblet's location.

"I will tell you that location, warrior, only after you hear what the curse did to me. Once you have heard, if you still want to find the goblet, I will tell you how. But if you are no fool you will turn back and tell Arthur you have failed."

Niall interrupts. "By the god to whom my people swear, I will *never* tell Arthur that I have failed. Not for as long . . ."

"Stop, Irishman," the body breaks in. "Your pride has nothing to do with this. The curse is far beyond mere mortal pride. Stop. And listen. My time is short.

"As a man I dreamt of many things, as men always do, but one dream came to me night after night for many years. In that dream a beast—I did not know what it was—would prowl my camp by night, raiding our food and killing: sometimes a horse, sometimes a woman, sometimes a man. Always it would approach my tent, and it would be black and surrounded by mist. It would reach for my tent and begin to open it . . . and just as it did so I would awaken.

"Then I learned of the goblet, and I spent all the time I could spare from fighting invaders trying to find it. I consulted priests, both Christian and Druid, and I asked many questions of Merlin, who was with me before he was with Arthur. Finally I found a scrap of the information I wanted, and I sent some men into the wilds to find out more. Whether or not they returned, I never found out.

"One night I dreamt my dream, but this time it was different. The beast came to my tent and began to open it, and I waited, as men do in a dream, to awaken. But suddenly the tent opened fully. The mists that surrounded the beast parted, and I saw the beast clearly for the first time. It was a bear—a huge, black bear—and it reached into my tent and clamped its massive arms around my head and pulled until all went dark.

"When I awoke I was here, and I knew I was dead. But my death did not bring peace, as in life I always hoped it would. Instead, I was still in the grip of the black bear, but now the bear had two human hands. Then I looked at the bear's face and in horror I saw that the face, too, was becoming human. Long I stared into that face and at those hands, and long the face stared back and the hands squeezed, until finally I knew.

"The face and the hands were mine."

Uther Pendragon falls silent. Niall waits, staring at the floor. The tomb is silent.

"Then, out of the corner of my eye, I saw my body lying on this stone slab where you found it. Slowly it dawned on me that what the bear was holding was not me, not my whole body, but only my head. Slower still, it came to me that the bear was turning—at least partly—into me. I screamed. For an eternity. Until my voice died at last."

The pause is leaden. Finally Niall speaks. "You terrify me, Uther Pendragon, but I see that you speak the truth. You say you have little time. Do you have time enough to allow me to make a decision?"

"Yes. A short time. But decide quickly, or I can no longer help you." With that, the body lies back down on the slab.

Niall sits in silence, thinking. Merely to know about the goblet, Uther says, is enough to trigger a ghastly curse. But not to know means failure, and that is a curse of another sort. There might be other ways of discovering the goblet without actually knowing its location, which perhaps would void the curse. Knowledge and curse? Or ignorance and no curse? That, it seems, is the choice.

If Niall asks Uther for the goblet's location, turn to section 47.

If he leaves without asking, turn to section 44.

AFTERWORD

WORKING WITHIN SOMEBODY else's secondary world (to use Tolkien's term) is almost as difficult as inventing your own. It shouldn't be. At least, that's what I kept telling myself as I worked through this book. David Drake's Arthurian England, it seemed to me, should be relatively easy to incorporate into a sequel because it is not a wholly invented world. Books of history, books of speculation, poems, novels, songs—all are available to the researcher. What, I asked myself, could possibly be left to the imagination?

Everything, as it turns out. Two problems became apparent right from the beginning. First was the staggering amount of research David Drake had done for *The Dragon Lord* itself. I don't think it's possible to read that novel without feeling somewhat in awe of the sheer realism of the setting. And I mean all aspects of that setting, from the vivid descriptions of landscapes to the detailed accounts of arms, armor, and buildings. Add to this Drake's obvious knowledge of the period's warfare and you have a very difficult act to follow.

The second problem, like the first, is reflected in Drake's introduction to this book. There are many literary sources for the Arthurian age and, in the end, many becomes too many: Chretien de Troyes, the *Gawain* poet, Thomas Malory, Alfred Lord Tennyson,

T. H. White, Marion Zimmer Bradley, Parke Godwin, and many anonymous authors. Where do you stop reading? All have different angles on the Arthur legend, and all are convincing in their own ways. The critic Harold Bloom has written of the anxiety of influence, where each writer tries to outwrite his or her predecessor. Surely, an author who attempts to retell the Arthurian sagas has as much anxiety as any author anywhere. There is just so much, and a lot of it is good.

I solved these two problems in the only way I knew. I couldn't match Drake's brilliant research, and the great quests had already been told, by authors far more able than I. After considerable anxiety and even more influence, I decided to write my own Arthurian story, sticking as close to Drake as I could but bringing in ideas that interest me. Where Drake is obviously fascinated by the history of the period, I am more interested in the legends, the myths. The question of Arthur's historical existence has never really concerned me, because he exists today. For me, that is all that matters. David Drake's detailed world is absorbing and brilliantly drawn, but my concern is with the Round Table and the Holy Grail. Once I realized that, things got a little easier.

I knew that I wanted to write about a quest for the Grail, but I wanted to avoid Arthur's legendary involvement in it, because Drake's Arthur is not the great, good prince of the early stories. My Arthur would want the Grail for selfish reasons, mostly to gain power. What power, though? First, the power to destroy the Saxons, thereby keeping the story inside Drake's realm. Second, the power to unite—in a sense—the old tribes and the new against the Saxons.

Arthur's role as a link between the ancient and the modern particularly interested me, especially since I had just finished reading Marion Zimmer Bradley's *The Mists of Avalon*. So I needed a Grail story that would link the old world with the new.

From there, it grew easier still. As I found out by looking at several books of mythology, the Grail is, in Christian legend, the cup used by Christ at the Last Supper, but variations of it exist throughout Celtic mythology. Arthur is supposed to have stolen a cauldron owned by Diwrnach the Irishman and, in a Welsh poem, he takes a cauldron from the lord of Annwn, the underworld. I decided to incorporate all of these themes into my story, but the real clincher was the cauldron of the god Bran. This cauldron restored the dead to life. Bran, also called the Blessed, was a patron of the arts and is the true and good King of Britain. His sister was Branwen (the daughter of Llyr), who tragically married the king of Ireland. Add the fact that the number three was important to both the Celts and the Christians; the idea that Bran was the original Fisher King (a name also applied to Christ); and the notion that Uther Pendragon, father of Arthur, is supposed to have been buried at Stonehenge, and you have the origins of my story.

Of course, the reader need know none of this. The background was necessary for me to provide a feel for the mythology. What I hope, above all else, is that the mythological basis of my story complements the extremely strong historical basis of David Drake's. If it does, and if it draws the reader back to the original book, then I have succeeded.

There were other considerations in the writing of

this book. The first was how to build in Mael and Starkad, *The Dragon Lord's* highly memorable major characters. I definitely wanted them in the story; readers of the original would feel cheated without them. So I gave them several major sections, trying to make their presence essential to the book's atmosphere. It's possible to avoid them, at least to some extent, but doing so robs the reader of an interesting part of the story.

The second problem was one I have noticed in many books of this type. I wanted to provide an enjoyable reading no matter which paths the reader chose. Multiple path books are by nature restrictive, demanding a certain course of action to achieve the desired ending. To a degree, this is unavoidable, but I wanted to allow several interesting ways of arriving at valid endings. The reader can miss large sections of text as a result of choosing a particular action, but it also means that the book can be re-read, I hope several times. That, I think, is the true wish of every author.

—Neil Randall

Neil Randall was born quite a few years ago in Kitchener, Ontario, Canada. Many things happened to him after that, but when all was said and done he had earned his Ph.D. in English literature and landed a job teaching Canadian literature and fantasy literature at the University of Waterloo, Canada. He promises he will not place his own book on his fantasy course.

At the age of fourteen, he had a letter published in a *Superman* comic book. This pleased him so much that he published nothing else for sixteen years. Since then, he has published four supplements for the *James Bond 007 Role-Playing Game:* "Octopussy," "Dr. No," "You Only Live Twice," and "Villains" (New York: Victory Games). With Greg Gorden, he designed *Monsters of Myth and Legend* for Mayfair Games of Chicago. He is also a regular software reviewer for *Compute!* magazine. He has a professional interest in the study of interactive fiction and is currently writing a book about this new genre.

CROSSROADS™ ADVENTURES

THE BEST IN FANTASY